T0107232

# Up Crabapple Creek

*Bernice Fishpaw*

iUniverse, Inc.
New York   Bloomington

Copyright © 2009 by Bernice Fishpaw

All rights reserved. No part of this book may be used or reproduced by
any means, graphic, electronic, or mechanical, including photocopying,
recording, taping or by any information storage retrieval system
without the written permission of the publisher except in the case
of brief quotations embodied in critical articles and reviews.
This is a work of fiction. All of the characters, names, incidents,
organizations, and dialogue in this novel are either the products
of the author's imagination or are used fictitiously.

iUniverse books may be ordered through booksellers or by contacting:

iUniverse
1663 Liberty Drive
Bloomington, IN 47403
www.iuniverse.com
1-800-Authors (1-800-288-4677)

Because of the dynamic nature of the Internet, any Web addresses or links
contained in this book may have changed since publication and may no longer be
valid. The views expressed in this work are solely those of the author and do not
necessarily reflect the views of the publisher, and the publisher hereby disclaims
any responsibility for them.

ISBN: 978-1-4401-1124-2 (sc)
ISBN: 978-1-4401-1125-9 (dj)
ISBN: 978-1-4401-1123-5 (ebook)

Library of Congress Control Number: 2009923030

Printed in the United States of America

iUniverse rev. date: 03/09/2009

# Chapter 1

"Hold still, Izzy!" Ma scowled.

"But you stuck me with a pin!" Izzy retorted, rubbing her arm.

"Well, if you'd hold still, I wouldn't stick you," Ma responded through the pins sticking out of her mouth.

Isabelle Norton stood on a chair, wearing one of Ma's old Sunday dresses, which had big red flowers on a blue background. Her two brown and yellow streaked braids of hair were fastened over her head with a bobby pin to keep them out of the way as Ma tried to shape the oversized dress to fit her skinny daughter.

"I liked this dress on you, but it makes me look like an old woman." Izzy made a face that Ma didn't see. "Why can't we buy a new dress for school from the Sears Roebuck catalogue?"

"We can't afford it. Just be happy with new shoes. Your pa had to borrow money from the bank to pay the taxes."

"Well, why can't I wear Bud's outgrown overalls, then?"

"You know good and well why. Girls are not allowed to wear overalls to school."

"Why?"

"The school won't allow it. Now, stand still, so I can get this dress to look halfway decent."

"Maybe I can wear last year's dress."

"Last year's dress is too tight. You're growing into a young lady now. Your breasts need room to grow."

"I don't want to be a young lady. I don't want my breasts to grow. I want to go to the university and learn to be an engineer, so I can invent stuff to make work easier."

"Now, Izzy, you know that's impossible. You are what you are. You're going to be a farmer's wife. You need to pay attention around here and learn how things get done, so you can become a good wife and mother. Now, stand still. I don't want to hear another word out of you."

# Chapter 2

"The calendar says today is a national holiday." Izzy wore the hated dress as she sulked at the breakfast table. "If Labor Day is a national holiday, why do they start school?"

"Every day is labor day on a farm," Pa declared. "We don't need to celebrate. The rest of the country is complaining about being out of work. Celebrating work seems out of place anyway." Pa sat at the head of the table, sipping a cup of coffee as he waited for Ma to bring his bacon, eggs, and potatoes. His faded bib overalls had patches on the knees and the seat.

Izzy's older brother, Bud, came into the kitchen. He wore brand new, long corduroy pants and a new shirt with a necktie. His brown hair glistened like patent leather from the all hair-glop. His last year's Sunday shoes were polished to a high shine.

"How come Bud gets new clothes to start school, and I have to wear this dumb dress?" Izzy asked.

Ma stood at the stove with her back to the table.

"Bud is going to be in high-school this year. There will be city kids there. He has to look good," Pa told her.

Bud defended himself. "I do the work of a hired man around here. I deserve something for that."

"Well, I do work, too, you know," Izzy replied.

Ma turned around with a platter of bacon and eggs. The look on her face told Izzy not to press the issue. *It just isn't fair*, Izzy thought.

"Thanks, Pa, for buying Mr. Turner's old, worn-out model 'T' truck." Bud wolfed down bacon and eggs. "My pal Andy O'Malley is a genius with cars. I learned a lot when he helped me fix her up. That old flivver runs as smooth as a new Buick now."

"Well, drive carefully, son. We don't have any insurance. And no racing."


Crabapple Creek School #8 and all the other one-room schools in county started on Labor Day. Except for having to wear the awful dress, Izzy looked forward to a new school year and all the wonderful things to learn. Seventh grade had lots of new scientific subjects such as anatomy and agriculture.

She packed a sandwich with butter and jelly, an apple, two homemade cookies, and a dill pickle in a gallon syrup pail. The tin cup with the initials "I. N." scratched on it sat on top of the food. It had been her school cup since first grade.

Izzy saw the Gruder family coming from the east. She hurried out to meet them. She carried last year's pencil box, which contained two new pencils, a penholder with two new pen points, and a new box of crayons with sixteen colors. She juggled all this with her dinner pail, half a bottle of ink, and a new tablet from The Mercantile.

Tucked safely in the tablet was last year's report card, just in case Miss Wagoner had forgotten that it said, "Promoted to seventh grade". She had skipped sixth grade.

The six Gruders had to walk two miles, the farthest of anyone at school. Jack was twelve, Izzy's age, and her best friend. He couldn't read and had repeated every grade. His younger sister, Irene, had passed him and would be in fourth grade. Now he would be in third grade with his sister Kitty.

Six-year-old twins, Maggie and Marie, joined their growing brood this year. At fifteen, Adele was still required by law to attend school. Big, strong and good-natured,

Dell found school learning hard and would only be in sixth grade.

"I hope Miss Wagoner will give us lots of new stuff to learn this year," Izzy confided to Jack as they hurried along.

"I wish I could just learn some of the old stuff." Jack sighed.

"Hey, you're not dumb. You just sometimes see letters backward is all," Izzy said.

The twins slowed down the whole procession. Marie begged Dell to carry her. They had already walked over a mile and a half, and a quarter of a mile still remained.

Dell picked up her little sister and sat her on her ample shoulders. Jack started to run before Maggie had a chance to ask him to carry her.

"I'll beat you to the front steps," he challenged to Izzy.

Her new shoes and all the supplies she carried slowed her down.

"Whoa! Look at that. Miss Wagoner must have a new car," Jack said. Izzy and Jack stopped in amazement. When they passed the row of lilac bushes that shielded the one-room, wooden school building by the creek, was a nifty, new, bright yellow Chevy roadster with a rumble seat, instead of Miss Wagoner's model 'T' runabout. They raced again, to see who would reach the new car first. It ended in a tie, just as it usually did.

Together, they burst through the front door of the, ancient, tiny building with the faded red paint peeling off, eager to congratulate their teacher on her new car, but stopped short. The woman writing on the blackboard with her back to the door couldn't be last year's teacher. She had written the words 'Miss Leona Webb'. Their noisy entrance turned her around.

A scowl of disapproval crossed her face. Younger and thinner than last year's teacher, her tight, yellow dress only reached her knees.

*Whew! I hope I didn't make a bad impression,* Izzy thought. Quickly, recovering from her shock, she volunteered to get a pail of water.

"Gee whiz, Izzy. Why did you go and do that?" gasped Jack, as she dragged him up the road to the O'Malley's well.

"Hey, did you see that look on her face? I had to do something quick to keep her from deciding she didn't like us."

# Chapter 3

Izzy hung the pail on the pump spout. "I think the school board should drill a well on the school grounds, so we wouldn't have to carry the water from the nearest farm."

"They probably can't afford it," Jack said, as he worked the pump handle up and down. "Maybe we could have a rain barrel, so we wouldn't have to come back at noon for more drinking water after everybody washed their hands. We got four rain barrels at our house, because we got such a big family. Rainwater is better for washing anyway."

Back at school, they poured the water into the big earthen jar with the spigot at the bottom.

"Hey, look. The first two seats on the big-kid row haven't been taken yet. You take the first one, Jack, and I'll sit behind you. I guess nobody wanted to sit in the front."

Jack put the remains of last year's tablet and a couple of short pencils with the erasers worn down to the tin, in the first desk. "I hope someone throws away a longer stub soon." Izzy pretended not to hear him.

Miss Webb rang the big bell in the cupola and waited for the noisy students to settle down.

Izzy looked around to see who sat behind her. Mike O'Malley, a redheaded boy with freckles, gave her a look that was a cross between a leer and a smirk. She stuck her tongue out at him.

"I hope you are ready for another year of learning," the new teacher said. "I will go over the rules only once. There will be no whispering, no gum chewing, and no walking around the room without permission. If you need to use the outhouse, you may do so if you raise your hand and show one finger. Do not make a habit of going during classes. That is what recess is for. If you need to use the dictionary or the encyclopedia, do it quietly and only one at a time. Are there any questions?"

Total silence followed.

"Good."

Eighteen curious faces looked at each other, unsure if they liked the new teacher.

*She sounds real mean,* Izzy thought. *I like the yellow dress, though. It matches her car, and I'll bet she has on lipstick and rouge. I wonder if she is a flapper. Ma's always going on about women in short dresses being flappers. I guess she thinks they are immoral or something.*

The door at the back of the room opened. Everyone turned around to see what was going on. Miss Webb scowled her annoyance.

"Yes?"

A tall, older woman in a long, black dress and a black straw hat stood in the doorway, holding the hand of a small boy hiding behind her. He wore knickers with stockings that had a pattern of different colored diamonds. His white shirt, buttoned at the neck, a bright blue bow tie and a vest looked out of place in the tiny country school. All the other boys wore faded bib overalls and blue cambric shirts. Everybody in the room stared. This kid looked strange to them.

But his strange clothing was not what got their attention. He wore thick glasses, which made his eyes look funny, and one eye seemed to be looking out the window. His head tipped to one side.

"Please, madam. I would like to enroll my grandson in your school."

"Does he live in the district?" Miss Webb inquired.

"Yes, madam, I have moved here from Chicago to keep house for Mr. Turner. Horace's mother died, and his father has disappeared. He is six years old and has been to kindergarten. He knows all his letters and numbers."

Maggie and Marie Gruder looked at the new boy with wide-eyed admiration, and they giggled. Miss Webb frowned at them. They quickly covered their mouths but stared. Some older students snickered. Miss Webb gave them a dirty look and assigned Horace a desk.

# Chapter 4

Last year's books from the book cupboard lay in separate stacks on the teacher's desk. "Your assignments for today are on the blackboard."

She called the roll, starting with first grade. Each student came to the desk and took the books she handed them. When she announced "sixth grade," Adele Gruder and Janet Andrews went to the desk.

Janet's long, blond curls hung down to her shoulders in graceful spirals like the fresh shavings from a wood plane. They stayed in place with a bright ribbon that matched the pretty dress she had on. Janet had at least five dresses and always wore a different one each day of the week. She made Izzy feel dowdy in her one made-over dress that she wore all week.

The teacher looked at the roster which Mr. Andrews, the school board chairman, had provided her. "Isabelle Norton, will you be joining us?" Her tone of voice made Izzy's hair crawl.

"But I'm in seventh grade." Izzy looked the teacher in the eyes as she responded from her desk.

"That is not what this roster says." Miss Webb's eyes locked on Izzy's.

"But right here on my last year's report card, it says 'Promoted to seventh grade.'"

"That must be a mistake."

"But . . ." There was a long pause. Everyone in the room looked at the teacher. Izzy looked away, found the card, and took it to the doubting Miss Webb.

Everyone looked at Izzy. *This horrible dress doesn't help.*

The silence ended when the new teacher finally spoke. "Very well, but you must know everything that is expected of a sixth grader. You will do seventh grade work and take seventh grade tests, but you will have to take and pass all sixth grade tests too." She handed her the sixth grade books. "I'll give you seventh grade books later."

Izzy went back and sat down at her desk. *Now I've done it. Ouch! I'll have to do twice as much studying. Okay. Whenever sixth grade is on the recitation bench, I'll just listen in like I did last year. I've got to show this old teacher that Izzy Norton is smarter than she, or anyone else, thinks.*

At recess, the Gruder twins escorted Horace to the playground and showed him the teeter-totter. The girls argued about who would sit with him on his half of the plank. Marie won. She and Horace sat almost in the middle of their end. The bigger Maggie sat at the very end of the other half of the plank, which hinged to the sawhorse in the middle. "I get to sit with Horace at noon," she hollered.

"Hey, necktie, where did you find that kid?" Mike jeered as the bell rang, calling the students in from recess.

"Four-eyes has got two girlfriends," Orville, a tall, gangling eighth grader added.

"Pick on someone your own size." Izzy kicked Orville in the shins.

He jumped around on one foot holding his leg. "Hey, what did I do? That kid gives me the creeps. City kids got no right to be in a country school. I bet he don't know a bull from a cow."

"Well, you probably don't know a street from an alley, and Mr. Turner pays taxes just like your pa, so he has as much right to be here as you do. If you do anything to hurt that kid, I'll knock you down and jump on you."

"Didn't your ma ever tell you not to fight with guys?" The argument ended when Miss Webb rapped her ruler on her desk.

# Chapter 5

The first day went from bad to worse. Mike jerked Izzy's pigtails. When she turned around and glared at him, Miss Webb saw her and scowled. Orville, sitting behind Mike, snickered. Mike pulled her hair harder. The teacher turned just then and caught him in the act. She made him trade seats with Jack. Then, Mike sat in the front row where the teacher could keep her eye on him.

"Serves you right," Izzy whispered just behind his ear.

Because they had carried the water in the morning, Jack and Izzy were assigned the water duty for the rest of the week. At noon, they had to go back to the well for another pail-full for the afternoon.

Everyone else had finished their dinners and had started a ball game by the time they finished eating. Without enough players for two teams, the game was "work-up." Only four players were at bat. Everyone else played in the field.

"Hey, you two slowpokes get in the outfield," Mike yelled to Izzy and Jack from the batter's box. On the very next pitch, he hit a fly ball in Izzy's direction. She ran to catch it, but her new shoes tangled in the grass, which had gotten long over the summer, and she fell flat on her face. Everybody laughed as she jumped up and ran the ball down. By that time, Mike had rounded the bases for a home run. "Thanks, Izzy," he taunted.

*I'll get you. You just wait and see,* Izzy silently vowed.

That afternoon all the students took their books home to create new dust covers from brown paper the first afternoon, Izzy cut some pretty pictures out of a magazine and pasted them on the front covers with paste made from flour and water. The next day, she saw Jack admiring her books as she tucked them into her desk. At recess, he asked if he could borrow her crayons. "Sure, as long as you don't break them."

Later that day, she noticed that Jack had drawn a beautiful picture of Miss Webb's new car on the cover of one of his books. *Jack might not be able to read, but he can draw better than anyone in the whole school.*

When the teacher saw the picture on Jack's book, she actually smiled. No one had seen her smile before. As soon as she realized that she had been caught smiling, she quickly frowned again and spoke sharply to Dell. "Quit chewing on your hair. Do you want to get hairballs like some old cat?"

# Chapter 6

Friday afternoon at three thirty, Miss Webb told them to put away their books for 'Friday Afternoon Society'. Friday Afternoon Society had been a part of school ever since Izzy could remember.

"We'll need officers for the new school year," the teacher announced. "Orville, because you were last year's president, please take your place and conduct this year's election." Orville was six feet tall, and his feet extended below his overall legs at least six inches. His voice sometimes went from low to a high squeak without any warning.

Orville reached into his desk, brought out a well-used hammer, and took his seat at the teacher's desk. He tapped lightly on the desk with a flourish, using the hammer for a gavel.

"Nominations are now open for president."

"Mr. President, I nominate Orville Brown," Mike said, before he could even be recognized.

"Mr. President, I object." Izzy jumped to her feet.

"On what grounds do you object?" Orville asked.

"He was president last year. Someone else needs a chance."

"Objection over ruled. Are there any other nominations?" Orville asked.

Jack stood up. "I nominate Izzy Norton."

"I object," Mike yelled.

"Why?" Orville asked.

"'Cause she's a girl, and girls can't be president. They're always secretary/treasurer."

"Where does it say that?" Izzy asked.

Orville looked at Miss Webb. The teacher appeared to be correcting papers at the back of the room and didn't look up. He suddenly found his hammer very interesting. He studied it a minute or two before he made a decision.

"We've never had this problem before, but I suppose every kid in this room can be president if he's the one the rest of the kids want. Are there any other nominations?"

"Mr. President, I move the nominations cease," Janet said. After five years, she knew all the special words for proper parliamentary procedure.

Orville and Izzy went outside, while the rest voted by raising their hands. The sixth graders counted the votes.

"Nine votes for Brown; eight votes for Norton," Janet announced when they returned.

*That figures. There are nine boys and eight girls. Jack probably voted for me, but it would be just like Janet to vote for Orville. She gets all gaga around the boys, especially Orville. Well, there is always next year,* Izzy thought.

The meeting proceeded. Mike was elected vice president and Izzy, secretary/treasurer.

With the new officers in place, they got down to the real business, which was electing duty officers for the following week. This included such positions as porch sweeper, two outhouse sweepers, (one boy and one girl), wood box filler, blackboard washer, eraser clapper, wastebasket dumper, two flag raisers, and the most important of all, the two water carriers.

Izzy groaned when they elected her to carry water for the second week in a row. But worse than that, they elected Mike O'Malley to be her partner.


She arrived at the schoolhouse a little early Monday morning. She picked up the pail and waited on the steps for Mike. Most of the students arrived—but not Mike. Being closest to the school, the O'Malley's allowed them to use their well. *I guess maybe I should just go meet him, or we'll be late,* Izzy thought.

She saw Mike come out of his house just as she arrived at the well.

"What took you so long?" she jawed. "You're supposed to do your share of this job."

"Awe ghee Izzy, it didn't hurt you any to bring the pail. It would be stupid for me to walk all the way to school and then have to walk back again just to bring the silly pail. I have to milk half a dozen cows every morning. You get off easy 'cause your old man has a milking machine."

"Well, your old man could have a milking machine, too, if he wanted one. That's no excuse for not doing your half of the work, carrying the water."

"My old man don't need no milking machine 'cause he's got six kids to do it." While Mike and Izzy argued, they filled the pail and carried it between them back to the school. Mike slopped some water on Izzy's leg. "Watch what you're doing," she snapped. Just as Izzy expected, the bell rang before the water was in the big jar. Miss Webb scowled.

After everyone had washed his or her hands for dinner, the water jar was nearly empty. Izzy had an idea. "Hey, Mike, I'll make you a deal. I'll get the water every noon, and you can take the pail home every night and bring it back full of water in the morning."

"Okay with me. I don't need no girl to help me anyway."

# Chapter 7

The weather was getting cold and nippy. When Izzy and the Gruders entered the building one morning, the strong smell of smoke and the odor of stove black greeted them. The stove black, put on in the spring to prevent rust, always stunk in the fall, the first time a fire was lit in the heating stove.

Miss Webb kept throwing paper through the open stove door, as smoke poured out. *I bet the teacher doesn't know much about operating a stove.* "Miss Webb, maybe if you opened the damper in the stovepipe and the draft, it would work better," Izzy suggested.

"Well, if you know so much about stoves, you can just start the fire." The teacher backed away and handed Izzy the Sears, Roebuck catalogue she had been tearing pages from. Good old Dell volunteered to get some kindling from the woodshed. Soon, the fire started burning, and warmth filled the room, welcoming the students after their morning walk in the frosty air.

Fall had arrived.

That afternoon, an emergency meeting of The Friday Afternoon Society elected a fireman. That had always been the teacher's duty before, but Miss Webb had other ideas. Izzy had no elected duty that week, so she became the unanimous winner to be the fireman. Her job included tending the stove, adding wood as needed, and keeping the draft and the damper adjusted to provide just the right amount of heat, so that it would not be too hot or too cold.

# Chapter 8

Saturday morning, Izzy found an old gunnysack in the shed. She bridled her black pony, Prince, and rode to the hickory nut tree in the woods, out of sight of the house. As they came around the corner of the woods, she saw an old car parked beside the road. She nudged the pony into a trot. When she rode into the woods, a man and a woman, with two little kids, picked up nuts from the ground.

"Go away," the man hollered. "We were here first."

"Well, you got no right to be here. My pa owns this land, and those nuts belong to us." The man started to swear, and he threatened Izzy with a big stick.

"My pa's a friend of the sheriff, and I'll call him up if you don't leave right now. I know the number on your license plate, and he'll come and arrest you."

The man swore some more and threw the stick at her. It hit Prince, just missing his eye. The pony reared up, and Izzy fell off, landing on her right shoulder.

At first she lay on the ground, stunned. Then, she realized that her right arm lay at a funny angle, and her fingers were numb. She couldn't move them.

"Prince! Where are you, Prince?" she called. Looking around, she saw a cloud of dust, as the car, with the man and his family, disappeared down the road. Then, she heard the galloping hooves of the pony, heading for the barn.

"Help!" Tears filled her eyes. "Oh please, God, help me!"

Izzy shivered. The cold, dark sky looked like it would bring snow any minute. *I've got to do something, or I'll freeze to death.* She rolled onto her knees. Holding her right arm against her body with her left hand, she was able to stand.

"Good heavens, Izzy, what on Earth happened?" Ma gasped as she walked into the kitchen.

"I fell off the pony. My arm is funny."

"Oh dear, Lord, What are we going to do? Pa's gone somewhere with the team, and Bud isn't home either. Ever since he got that rickety old truck, no one ever knows where he is. We've got to get you to the doctor." Ma rang up Dr. Hull on the telephone.

"He says if I can bring you right in, he'll take care of you. Now, I wish I'd learned how to drive a car." Ma twisted her apron into a tight knot.

"I know how to drive, Ma."

"You can't possibly drive with a broken arm."

"No. But I know how, and I can tell you how."

"Well, I'm not sure, but I guess we'll have to give it a try."

Seated next to Ma in the passenger seat of their open touring car, Izzy told her mother, step-by-step, just what to do. The engine started, but when Ma had shifted the lever on the floor into reverse and let out the clutch, it promptly died. It took three tries before they finally backed out of the shed. Getting into low was a little jerky, but by the time they reached the end of the driveway, it moved a little more smoothly.

Izzy showed Ma how to steer and helped with her good left arm. Soon, they were rolling along the road. They managed to get into second gear with Ma's foot on the clutch and Izzy's left foot on the gas pedal and her left hand moving the shift lever. "We better not try to get into high."

The speedometer read fifteen miles an hour. Izzy figured it should take about twenty minutes to go the five miles to Wilton.

"To slow down, you just put the right foot on the brake a little, and to stop, put your feet on the clutch and the brake at the same time." Izzy forgot all about her wounded arm, which Ma had tied to her body with a dish towel.

# Chapter 9

"I don't think it's broken," Doctor Hull said, as he studied the wounded Izzy after her coat and shirt had been removed. She sat on the table, bare to her waist, her budding breasts showing. *This is so embarrassing.* "But the shoulder is dislocated and will have to be put back in the socket."

The nurse gave Izzy a shot in her left arm.

"Miss Arnison is going to give you a little gas to breathe so you can relax," the doctor told her.

A sharp odor hit Izzy when the black rubber mask covered her nose and mouth. Ma held her left hand.

"Be brave, Izzy," she whispered in her ear. "I love you."

Izzy moved her head right, then left, trying to get away from the stink, but the mask just stayed in place. She held her breath, but at last she gasped, and everything seemed to be going around in circles.

The doctor took off his shoe and put his heel into her armpit and pulled the arm.

When she woke up, he was moving the arm up, down, and around. "Can you move your fingers?" he asked. Izzy blinked and tried to move the fingers. To her surprise, all five of them responded, but her whole arm ached something awful.

"You'll need to wear this strange contraption for a couple weeks," the doctor told her, as he adjusted a padded aluminum splint around her chest and arm. Bent at the elbow and wrapped with a stretchy bandage, the arm stuck out at a right angle from her body. "It's called an airplane splint," the doctor explained.

Izzy tried to joke. "I always wanted to fly. Now I have my first wing."

Ma gave the doctor a ten-dollar bill. She buttoned her own coat around Izzy as best she could and draped Izzy's dirty coat over her own shoulders. When they opened the door, big snowflakes blew into their faces from the dark sky. A half-inch of snow already covered the ground.

"I can't do it. I can't possibly drive that car home in the snow, and you half-asleep" Ma said. They retreated into the warm waiting room.

Izzy had never been so glad to see Bud as when he walked into the doctor's waiting room, followed by Pa. Even Ma agreed that Bud's flivver came to the rescue. "We saw your note on the kitchen table," Pa told them.

Seated next to Ma in the backseat of the car with a blanket wrapped around them, Izzy dozed off, feeling closer to Ma than she had for a long, long time. The shot had done its job.

# Chapter 10

Izzy could not remember such a long night. The clock downstairs bonged each hour. *Is this night ever going to end?* The bitter little pill the doctor had given her to take at bedtime had dulled the pain at first, but now it had worn off, and the pain came back. She lay on her back, the wounded arm in the aluminum splint pointing straight at the ceiling in the cold bedroom. She tried sleeping on her left side, but her arm stood straight out and started to throb. Then, she tried lying on her tummy with the arm hanging over the side of the bed. That didn't work either.

At last, she got up, slipped her feet into her slippers, and groped her way to the kitchen. With her left hand, she lit the kerosene lamp. She put a kerosene-soaked corncob in the cook stove and added wood to start a fire. Her right arm tried to help the left arm but couldn't. Sitting at the kitchen table, looking into the flickering lamp, her mind wandered back to yesterday.

"Why did I have to be so selfish?" Izzy wondered out loud. "I should have just let them have the old nuts. They're probably so poor that those nuts would have been the only good thing those little kids would get to eat. Now, the snow has covered them up, and nobody will get them."

Daylight finally streamed into the kitchen. The snow had stopped falling and had crusted the yard, leaving the brown weeds showing through. Ma came into the kitchen. "It's time to take another pill." Ma took the last pill from the tiny bottle and gave it to Izzy with a glass of water.

"Thank you, Lord, that Izzy was not hurt worse than she was," Pa prayed before breakfast. Eating with her left hand seemed awkward, and Izzy didn't feel hungry.

"Can I be excused from church? I have homework to do. It will take longer with my right hand sticking out like a dead stick I'll have to write with my left hand." She looked at Ma, who nodded agreement.

Monday morning, Ma told her that she didn't need to go to school. "But I can't miss a single day. I have to pass every test the sixth graders take, or Miss Webb will put me back, and I can't stay in seventh grade."

"Hey, Crip!" Bud teased. "If you hurry up, I'll give you a ride on my way to school."

Wrapped in Ma's shawl, Izzy discovered she could hang her dinner pail on the end of the metal splint. Her left arm clutched her books as she gingerly climbed down from the worn seat of the ancient truck.

The heating stove crackled a warm greeting .*I'm glad I don't have to take care of the stove this week.* When the other students arrived, Izzy became the center of attention. Everyone wanted to know what happened. The story improved each time she told it. Suddenly, Izzy Norton became a folk hero. She had driven away the evil nut thieves from the city.

Jack even offered to do her writing. Knowing how Jack got everything backward, she refused the offer. Trying to write with her left hand, she discovered that some of her letters came out backward too, and her hand smeared the ink.

Only Janet failed to tell her how wonderful and courageous she had been. Instead, she ignored the chattering students and pretended to find something in the encyclopedias.

*Ghee, do you suppose Janet is jealous?* Izzy wondered.

# Chapter 11

"Tap, tap, tap." Orville rapped the hammer/gavel on the teacher's desk. "Friday Afternoon Society will come to order."

After the regular business of electing the duty officers for the following week completed, he asked for new business.

"Mr. President." Kitty Gruder, a third grader, stood up.

"The chair recognizes Miss Gruder."

"Are we going to have a Halloween program and box supper this year?"

Everyone looked at Miss Webb, who sat at the back of the room on a chair reserved for visitors. She only advised 'The Friday Afternoon Society'. "Mr. President, I suggest that you poll the organization to see if they wish to have a program and box supper."

"Okay, everyone in favor of a program, raise your hand," Orville said. All hands waved in the air.

"Because every activity that takes place in this school is supposed to be a learning experience, I propose that The Friday Afternoon Society be the sponsors for the event," the teacher told them.

"We've never done that before," Dell said. Everyone looked at each other.

Soon, everyone was talking at once. Finally, Orville tapped the hammer/gavel on the desk and called for order. "What do I do now?" he asked, looking straight at the teacher.

"Appoint a committee."

"Okay, I appoint Janet Andrews to be the chairman. Miss Andrews, you can select anyone you want to be on your committee."

Janet gave Izzy one of her sweet, superior smiles that Izzy hated. She always felt that Janet was making fun of her dress. "I appoint Izzy, Dell, and Mike. Orville will be an automatic member because he's the president," Janet declared.

The following Monday, Miss Webb announced that sixth, seventh, and eighth grade language classes would be combined, and that half hour would be used to plan the program.

"Well, the little kids can each say a piece. Each of them can pick some rhyme they like and memorize it," Janet stated. The committee squeezed onto the recitation bench, while she stood in front of them.

"We'll need some songs," suggested Orville.

"Okay, you're in charge of picking out the songs and leading the singing," Janet directed.

"We need to have a play of some sort," Izzy added.

"Yah, it needs to be something real scary, too, 'cause it's Halloween," said Mike.

"It can't be more than twenty minutes," Janet commented. "People will be getting hungry."

"We could do 'The Legend of Sleepy Hollow'. That's scary," Izzy suggested. The sixth grade had just finished studying the story.

"Izzy, that's dumb," Janet said, looking down her nose.

Izzy defended the idea. "No, it isn't."

"Okay, if you think it's such a good idea, then you can be the director. You can report on how we can do it at our meeting tomorrow."

Izzy took her American literature book home that night and re-read The Legend of Sleepy Hollow. *I should have kept my mouth shut,* she thought. *How can we possibly make any sense of this story in twenty minutes?*

She couldn't sleep for thinking about the problem. By the time she heard the big clock downstairs strike four, she had a plan. She laid it out for the committee that afternoon.

"The front of the room will be our stage. We can run a wire from the tops of the window frames on each side, to hold a curtain like in a theater. I'll bring Pa's Coleman lantern and our gasoline mantle lamp. They're really bright and will be sort of like footlights in the front of the stage area."

"Where are you going to get a curtain?" Janet asked.

"Well, if each of us can borrow a sheet from our mothers, we can hang them from a wire with safety pins."

"But that story takes place in three or four different places. We can't make scenery and stuff." Janet frowned and shook her head. "We want everything to be perfect."

"The way I figure it, the main scene will be the party at the Van Tassel home. We can put a tablecloth on the teacher's desk for the refreshment table, and the recitation bench can be a sofa if we cover it with a blanket and a pillow or two. Orville can be Icabod Crane, and Mike can be Brom Bones. Everyone else will be a guest. The girls can borrow dresses from bigger girls to make them look like old-time long dresses. We can make cardboard knee buckles covered with tinfoil gum wrappers for the boys. They'll be wearing their Sunday knickers anyway. Even men used to wear knickers in the olden days. I'll be Katrina." Izzy stopped to get her breath.

"Oh no, you can't be Katrina. There's nothing in the story about a broken arm. I think I should be Katrina," Janet declared. "She's supposed to be beautiful." She tossed her head to flourish her golden curls.

"The splint is coming off before Halloween," Izzy retorted.

"The story says Katrina was plump as a partridge," Dell put in. "How are you going to look plump?"

"I forgot about that." Janet looked confused for a few seconds but quickly recovered. "I can just tie a pillow around my waist and borrow one of my granny's big dresses."

"All right, then I'll be the mistress of ceremonies," Izzy agreed reluctantly.

"Hey, how about me?" Orville interrupted. "I'm the president."

"You're Ichabod," Izzy reminded him. "You can be the auctioneer after the program."

"Okay, Izzy, what will you do for that scene where Brom Bones chases Ichabod and throws his head at him?" Mike asked.

"I thought about that. To start the play, I'll stand in front of the curtain and read parts of the story explaining about the valley and the new teacher. Everyone will be in place at the party when the curtains open. The boys will be on one side. Brom Bones tells the story about the headless horseman. Make it really scary, Mike. The girls will be gathered around the table, dipping up punch from a crock.

Dell can be Mrs. Van Tassel, and she'll ask Ichabod to sing a song. After the song, the fiddler will start to play, and all the guests will start to dance."

"Hey, wait a minute. Where're you going to get a fiddler?" Mike asked.

"Guess what? Ma was over to old man Turner's the other day to welcome his new housekeeper with a pie. Horace was practicing on his violin. Ma said he sounded pretty good too. Seems his mother played violin in some fancy orchestra in Chicago before she died. Maybe he can play 'Turkey in the Straw' or something."

"But we still haven't gotten to the scary part," Mike complained.

"Well, Katrina will flirt with Ichabod, and Brom will act jealous. He'll slink away while the dance is still going on. Then, all the guests will leave, and the curtains will close." We can move the lantern and lamp to the back of the stage, and Ichabod and Brom can ride back and forth between the lights and the closed curtains on cardboard horses, so only their shadows will show to the audience. Jack's a good artist. He can make the horses from some old cardboard boxes and broom handles."

"It all sounds dumb to me. Everyone will know they're not real horses," Janet argued.

"Of course, they'll know, but they'll know its all make-believe anyway, and shadows will be spooky, especially since Mike will have his jacket over his real head, to make him look headless. Jim and Harry can be off to the side, away from the lights and beat on an empty cardboard box with a couple sticks of kindling to make it sound like horses' hooves. We can even have Brom throw a pumpkin for his head at Ichabod."

"It still sounds dumb," Janet protested.

# Chapter 12

Bud taunted his sister: "Hey, Dizzy Izzy, I hope whoever buys your box doesn't get food poisoning."

"Go jump in the creek," she snapped and stuck her tongue out at her brother.

"Touchy! Touchy! You're nervous as a cat in a thunderstorm."

"Pa, make him leave me alone."

"Just relax. Everything will work out okay," Pa assured her.

"But dress rehearsal was a disaster. The curtain got stuck, Jim and Harry couldn't make the box sound like horses, and Mike left out the most important part of the story. Then he got mad when I made him do it over. Only Janet and Orville's dancing seemed to go right. Janet flirted with the big oaf, and he ate it up."

Izzy helped Ma put special food in the two boxes they had decorated for the occasion. Izzy had even saved the waxed paper from the inside of the cornflake box, to wrap the angel food cake and the fried chicken. Two dishes of potato salad, baked beans, and cottage cheese went into each box. Ma's cottage cheese had a reputation as the best in the county.

Bud filled the Coleman lantern and the mantle lamp with fresh gasoline and pumped them up. The four kerosene lamps at the school didn't make enough light to even recognize someone ten feet away.

"Do you have any idea what Janet's sister's box will look like?" Bud asked.

"I wouldn't tell you if I did," Izzy said.

"I wouldn't mind getting one of the Andrews' boxes, myself," Pa offered. "Annabelle Andrews is one of the best cooks in the county. I love her Swedish meatballs and her rice pudding topped with lingonberries. Umm! Umm!" Ma gave him a rap on the knuckles with the back of a fork as he reached for a piece of chicken.

"Those Swedish spritz cookies with all those spices are pretty damn good too," Bud added. Ma scowled. Ma always scowled when Bud used bad words.

# Chapter 13

Some people had already arrived when the Nortons entered the tiny building with the bright lights. Every family brought folding chairs, which were set in back, behind the rows of desks. The students sat double in the two rows of little desks, to make room for the audience.

The lamp and the lantern, placed on two of the front desks, with cookie pans behind them for reflectors, lit the stage area. The dictionary table in the back corner filled up with brown paper bags holding the decorated boxes.

At exactly eight, by the octagonal clock on the wall over the blackboard, Orville stood up and cleared his throat. The little room hushed. "Ladies and gentlemen, tonight we present a program for your pleasure. Janet Andrews is the producer/chairman, assisted by her committee of Michael

O'Malley, Adele Gruder, and Isabelle Norton. We hope that you will enjoy it."

*So far—so good,* Izzy thought.

The curtain opened just wide enough for all nineteen students to stand without showing the furniture at the sides. They sang a rousing rendition of 'She'll Be Comin' 'Round the Mountain', followed by 'Casey Jones' and 'My Darling Clementine'. Orville's voice didn't crack even once. Singing seemed to work better for him than just plain talking.

The Gruder twins were cute when they spoke their piece together, but they couldn't be heard beyond the front row. Every kid recited a favorite poem. At last, it was time for the climax—the play. The twins closed the curtains without any problems. While the rest of the cast went behind the curtain and put on their costumes, Izzy stood in front, telling the story about the place called Sleepy Hollow and how a young man named Ichabod Crane came to be the teacher at the little school.

When she gave the signal to the twins, the curtains parted to reveal the Van Tassel party. The boys, wearing their Sunday knickers with big, shiny cardboard buckles on their knees, stood at one side. Jack, as Mr. Van Tassel, sat on the bench, which had been turned into a sofa. He had a brown beard fashioned from corn silks, and he pretended to smoke a corncob pipe.

Mike told the tale about how a headless horseman roamed the area. He made it sound very scary, especially the part about the horseman who rode around during the full moon, looking for his head.

Orville wore last year's Sunday long pants, so his legs showed more than usual above his ankles, and his arms hung out below his sleeves.

The girls, in long dresses, gathered around the table and dipped apple juice punch from a crock into their school cups. Dell, as Mrs. Van Tassel, had flour in her hair to make her look old. She clapped her hands together for attention and announced that Mr. Crane had agreed to sing a solo.

Orville strutted forward and gave a rendition of 'The Old Oaken Bucket' so well, the audience all clapped. *The song probably hadn't been written at the time of the play, but nobody knows the difference.*

Katrina looked very plump in her granny's dress with the pillow under it. She flirted by making eyes at Ichabod, while slyly looking to see if Brom was watching.

Horace plucked his fiddle two or three times before he started playing 'Turkey in the Straw'. *Everything is going well.* The little fellow got into the spirit of the play, and all the dancers hopped around to the beat.

Even the audience began to clap to the music. They had planned to play the tune three times, but everyone seemed to be having such a good time, so Izzy prompted Horace from the side to keep playing. Katrina and Ichabod bounced the hardest, and the pillow started to droop until it dragged on the floor. Orville tripped on it and fell right on top of Janet. Horace's eyes grew bigger than usual behind his thick glasses, and he stopped playing.

Dead silence followed for two or three seconds, and then everyone in the house started to laugh. Everyone roared except Janet and Orville. Izzy tried hard not to laugh.

Janet picked up the pillow and hit Orville over the head with it. Orville made a dash for the door at the back of the room. Janet ran after him, waving the pillow over her head.

Izzy tried to be serious long enough to announce a fifteen-minute intermission. Most of the men and boys went outside.

"Wow, what a perfect ending," Dell and Izzy laughed to each other.

Janet gave up the chase at the door and ran behind the curtain behind the stove. They were sure she was crying, but neither had enough courage to console her.

# Chapter 14

"I'm hungry," Dell declared. "Let's set up for the auction."

Izzy and Dell, with Miss Webb, carried the decorated boxes to the front of the room. They removed the brown paper bags and stacked the boxes on the teacher's desk. The girls' boxes went on one end and ladies' boxes on the other.

The pretty boxes, covered with colored crepe paper and a great variety of paper flowers and bows, hid mysterious and tempting food. Six boxes of different sizes, covered with white paper decorated with crayon pictures, left no doubt that Jack had decorated the Gruder ladies' entries. Dell put the prettiest girls' box, wrapped in blue satin with a pink organdy bow, behind all the others.

Soon, the men and boys returned to the little schoolroom. Orville swaggered in like some sort of a hero. Izzy handed him his hammer/gavel.

The girls' boxes sold first. "There is a twenty-five cent limit on student boxes," Orville announced. Izzy, as treasurer, collected the money. Dell held up the first box, with the picture of a small boy with a bow tie and glasses playing a violin drawn on the cover. She tipped it up so everyone could see the picture. Right off, Horace bid five cents. Mike bid ten. *He doesn't really want to eat with a first grader. He must think it's fun to bid the price up on the little city kid.* When it got to twenty-five cents, Horace came up, paid his quarter, and took his box.

The next box had a picture of a small boy in glasses and two girls on the teeter-totter. *Jack is one good artist,* Izzy thought. Again, Horace bid a nickel. Mike again bid a dime. Horace looked disappointed but did not raise the bid. No one else bid. Mike had bought the other twin's box. Izzy took his dime and muttered under her breath as he paid her, "It serves you right."

One by one, all the boxes sold. Mike offered to sell Horace the box he didn't really want for a dime. Horace shook his head, because he didn't have a dime. Mike settled for a nickel.

Only two boxes remained when the blue and pink box came up. Janet looked up from her pout for the first time. Mike bid fifteen cents. Orville banged the hammer/gavel.

"The auctioneer bids twenty-five cents," Orville said, just as his voice squeaked. "Sold."

Only Izzy's box remained. Mike muttered, "Five cents."

"I have five cents; do I hear ten?" chanted the auctioneer. No one spoke. All the other boys had already made their purchases.

# Chapter 15

Orville opened the meeting Friday afternoon.

After the routine business was finished, he said, "Everyone wants to know what we should do with the money from the box supper."

"How much did we make?" Dell asked.

"Seventeen dollars and twenty-seven cents," treasurer Izzy told them.

Mike spoke up first. "We should get some chicken wire and make a backstop for the ball field. Then we wouldn't waste so much time running down foul balls and wild pitches."

"That's a lousy idea. I think we should buy a Victrola and some classical records," Janet said. She looked straight at Izzy. "We need a little more class around here."

"That costs too much," Izzy said. "We need a well, but drilling a well costs too much too."

"Maybe we could get gutters and rain barrels to collect water for washing our hands," Jack said.

"Rain barrels breed mosquitoes," Jim put in. "And we'd still have to carry water to drink."

Harry suggested getting a big milk can that they could pull in a wagon. "Maybe, that way, we could make only one trip a day to the well."

"Who is strong enough, besides me, to lift a five-gallon can of water into the water jar?" Orville asked. "I ain't gonna do that every day, and I'm gonna graduate and won't be here next year."

Orville asked for a show of hands on each idea. None of the ideas received a majority.

Izzy called to be recognized. "I move we table the question to a later meeting. Maybe something will come up that we can all agree on."

That motion carried. "Miss Webb can lock the money in her desk drawer." The president banged his hammer. "The meeting is adjourned."

# Chapter 16

A couple weeks later, before classes started one morning, Miss Webb asked the whole school, "What holiday is next week?"

"Thanksgiving," they all called at once.

"Each of you will stand up in turn and tell us one or two things that you are thankful for this year." The teacher looked around the room. "We will start with Orville."

Orville stood up and looked at the floor. "Well, I wasn't expecting the question, so I don't know the right answer offhand. I'll pass." He sat down.

"Isabelle?"

Izzy stood up. "I'm like the pilgrims. I'm thankful for the harvest. We have a barn full of hay, oats in the granary for our cows and horses, and corn in the crib for the pigs and chickens. Besides, we have hundreds of jars of fruit and vegetables in the cellar and a big bin full of potatoes, so we'll eat this winter."

"Janet?"

"I'm thankful that my father bought land instead of stocks. That way, we didn't lose anything in the big crash. And Grandpa Peterson's bank in Chicago didn't have to close either," she added.

They went around the little room as each student stood and told what they were thankful for. Finally, it was Horace's turn. Even after his success at the Halloween program, he still seemed shy. He stood up, though, looking at his feet, and he spoke a little louder than he usually did. "I'm thankful that Mr. Turner gave me and Granny a warm place to live and plenty of food to eat. He even buys the food and pays Granny something."

Horace raised his eyes and looked at Miss Webb. "My father went to another city to look for work. He never came back, and then Mother died." He looked at his feet again. When he looked up, there were tears in his eyes. "The landlord of the apartment we lived in told Granny if she didn't pay the rent we had to get out."

When he looked up at the teacher, she nodded and smiled at the timid child. He looked around and saw everyone in the room looking at him. Some looked sad; others let their mouths hang open. He looked straight at different students.

"We had spent every cent Granny had saved. I though we would have to live under a bridge in a cardboard box."

As he looked at each of his schoolmates, he spoke a little louder. They wanted to know more. "Granny went to Janet's grandpa's bank to see if she could borrow some money. He told her about an old man in Wisconsin. He said Mr. Turner needed someone to keep house for him because his wife had died. Her grandpa and grandma even brought us to Wisconsin with their car."

Everyone looked at Horace in astonishment. Except for the twins, no one else had heard him talk this much since he had come to Crabapple Creek. Now the words fell from his mouth.

He told about some of his friends whose fathers had jumped out of high buildings and had died. He told about the long bread lines where men and women lined up for hours to get a slice of bread and a bowl of soup.

Miss Webb let him talk.

When he was finished, Irene Gruder raised her hand. "Maybe that's what we should do with our $17.27. We can give it to Janet's grandpa to help some little kids in Chicago." Everyone agreed.

# Chapter 17

Orville banged on the teacher's desk with his hammer and called for order.

After routine business, he asked, "Does anybody have any neat idea for Christmas? Miss Webb made us do the Halloween program, so she probably expects us to do Christmas too."

"The teachers always planned a program before, and Santa Claus comes, and we draw names and exchange gifts." Mike said. "She should do it this year too."

Everyone turned around and looked at Miss Webb. She smiled and shook her head from side to side. It was the reaction everyone expected.

Orville heaved a big sigh. "Okay, I guess we better get on with it."

"Halloween was a disaster," Janet said. Everyone else snickered.

Even Orville grinned a little. "So, let's hear any ideas the rest of you have."

"We can't have Christmas without Santa Claus," Mike said, "At least for the little kids."

"Before he left to find work and never came back, my father told me that Santa Claus lost everything he had when the stock market crashed. Father said Santa retired and moved to Florida," Horace told them.

Maggie, the larger and more talkative twin, said, "My sister Kitty says there ain't no Santa Claus. She said she saw Ma and Pa putting the presents under our tree last year and then told us that Santa brought them."

"I think Christmas is a good time to send our Halloween money to some kids in Chicago that live in cardboard boxes under bridges like Horace thought he would have to do," Irene added.

"I think we need a committee, just like at Halloween," Izzy said.

"Okay, if you want a committee, I appoint you as chairman," Orville said, pointing at Izzy with the handle of his hammer. "You can choose your committee."

"Well, let's see . . . I'll pick Janet and,"

"Oh no, you won't. I don't want any part of your harebrained ideas. Count me out." Janet twisted her face in distaste and stuck out her tongue.

"Ooohhh-kay. Dell, Jim, and Irene, Jack, Mike, " Izzy looked around the room, "and Horace."

"Horace's only a first grader and a city kid at that," Mike protested.

"He can represent the little kids. He might surprise us with some new ideas," Izzy said.

Monday at noon, Izzy and her committee met in the front of the room, while the rest of the school ate their dinners sitting around in the back. Izzy read off the list on her tablet, "Number one, Santa Claus."

"If Maggie and Marie and Horace don't believe there's a Santa Claus, I don't know if we even need one. They're the littlest kids," Irene said.

"Okay, scratch old Santa Claus." Izzy drew half a dozen long dashes through the word Santa Claus on her tablet. "Number two, Christmas tree,"

"They sell pretty ones, tall and full, at The Mercantile for only a dollar. We can take some of the box supper money and get a nice one," Jim suggested.

"Oh no," Irene interrupted. "We're going to send that money to Chicago for little kids living under bridges in boxes."

"If we had some colored chalk, I could draw a really neat Christmas tree on the blackboard," Jack told them.

"White chalk should be okay," Horace put in. "It would look like snow."

"Good idea. How will we decorate it?" Izzy asked, as she put a check after the word "tree" on her tablet.

"Maybe everyone in school can draw and color an ornament or two on paper, and we can paste them on the tree," Jack said.

"That leaves entertainment and refreshments." Izzy wanted to keep the meeting moving.

"I had to learn 'The Night before Christmas' for my ma's club last year. I'll brush up on it," Jim said. Jim was in fifth grade.

"It would be fun to have a Santa Claus come out of a fireplace and fill some stockings while Jim recites it," Irene suggested. "Jack can make us a fireplace out of a big box, and we can have Santa come out of the box. Orville's voice is deep enough now that he can let out a good 'Ho-ho-ho'."

"I'm not sure I can find a box big enough for Orville to get through and still have room for some stockings and stuff," Jack objected.

Horace bounced up and down with his hand in the air. "I know! I know! I can be Santa Claus. I'm small, and I can 'Ho-ho-ho' just as good as Orville. See—'Ho-ho-ho'." He made his voice really deep.

They all laughed and agreed. "That would be entertaining and fun. For his round little belly that shook like jelly, we can use a sofa pillow, and we'll be sure it doesn't fall out. We'll sew strings at the top to hang around his neck like an apron," Izzy said, as everyone laughed, remembering Janet at Halloween.

"Songs—we need Christmas songs. Can you do the songs again, Orv?" Izzy asked.

"I don't think so," Orville replied. "My voice does crazy things. I just don't trust it."

"Did you know Harry is the lead soprano and soloist in our boys' choir at church?" Irene asked. "He's good. Let's ask him to lead the singing." Harry was a fourth grader. "There are lots of Christmas Carols. I love Christmas Carols."

Izzy made a note to talk to Harry. "Does anyone think we should try to do the real Christmas story?" she asked. They agreed by nodding their heads.

"I think its best straight from the Bible. Janet's a good reader. Maybe she would get out of her grouch long enough to read it while the rest of us could be Mary and Joseph, the wise men, angels, shepherds, and innkeeper," Dell said.

"That would be a lot of work, getting costumes and stuff," Izzy said.

"Those Bible people just wore long stuff. Maybe we can use long nightshirts," Irene suggested. "We can put dish towels around our heads and tie them on with neckties or use some rope for belts."

For refreshments, I'll ask Ma to let me make cookies. There's enough ice in the creek now that we can make two or three freezers of ice cream. Maybe Dell and Irene can make the custard.

Dell nodded okay.

"The guys can chop some ice from the creek and turn the freezers."

"Gifts—we need to draw names to exchange gifts," Jim said.

"I have a better idea," Irene interrupted. "Instead of giving each other some silly little cheap thing, we could each throw in a quarter with the Halloween money for the poor little kids in Chicago."

"I think the whole school needs to decide that." Orville showed his presidential authority.

"It's almost one o'clock—time to get back to school stuff." Izzy slammed the lid back on her dinner pail. "We'll ask Miss Webb to give us time each day to get the rest of the kids into the planning and to practice."

# Chapter 18

Everybody cheered when Miss Webb said they could have a whole hour after dinner every day to get ready for Christmas. They got right to work.

Janet flatly refused to be the reader. "Absolutely not. I will not take part in any play produced by a bunch of kids. If the teacher can't be bothered to supervise, I won't be bothered either," she told Dell.

"Maybe Mike could read," Izzy suggested, when Dell told her that Janet had refused. "He's Catholic, but I think it's the same Bible and the same story, isn't it?"

"Okay," Mike agreed, when Izzy asked him. "You'll have to pick out the parts to read though, and be sure there are not too many hard words."

Harry said he had a Christmas songbook at home and would bring it to help pick out the songs.

"I want to be Mary!" Irene said. "I know just what I can wear. Our baby doll at home can be Baby Jesus. It's worn and has lost an arm, but when it's wrapped in swaddling clothes, no one will notice."

"Hey, I know what," Horace shook his arm over his head. "We've got a real Joe to be Joseph." Joe was in fourth grade and the same size as Irene.

He looked a little surprised at Horace's suggestion. "What do I have to do?"

"You don't have to learn any lines or do anything, because Mike is going to read the story. You just lead the donkey and knock on the inn door, then take Mary back across the stage to the barn. Joseph was a good husband, so I think he probably got some fresh straw for her to lie on and covered it with his coat," Izzy told him.

"Hey, I put down bedding for the cow every day at home. I can do that." Joe's face turned red, but from his smile, everyone knew he was happy to have such an important part.

They selected Orville, Jim, and Jack to be the wise men since Mike would be reading.

"The rest of the kids can be the choir and the angels and shepherds and stuff. We'll work the right carols into the story at the right time. Harry, write down the names of the songs you want." Izzy smiled. *This is easier than I thought. We will leave out the part about the mean king killing all the baby boys. That doesn't seem right for Christmas, even if it is in the Bible.*

"Don't forget about 'The Night before Christmas,'" Jim reminded Izzy.

"You said you knew the piece. Right off, it says 'Mama in her kerchief and I in my cap'. . . Dell, can you be Mama? You'll be lying on a blanket sleeping. A bed would be too much trouble. You can wear a big nightshirt over your clothes. Maybe your stocking cap would look like a pointed nightcap," she told Jim.

"To start, when the curtain opens everything would be dead quiet. You roll over and face the audience, leaning on your elbow, and say the first line. Offstage, some of the guys will make a racket when you get to that part. When Santa Claus crawls out of the fireplace with a gunny sack, he'll laugh and fill stockings, then crawl back in. From behind the curtain, he'll call, 'Merry Christmas to all, and to all a good night.'"

That weekend, Orville and Mike begged for some big cardboard boxes from The Mercantile.

The next week, everyone had fun making tree decorations and angel wings. For the three wise men's gifts, they polished a brass bowl for the gold, Orville brought one of his mother's fancy cologne bottles for the frankincense, and Jim brought their vinegar cruet for the myrrh.

Jack used up half of Izzy's crayons making the manger and some animals, which he nailed on wide boards to make them stand up.

Orville added cross-wires to the long curtain wire that was still fastened to the tops of the window frames from Halloween. A sheet on each of these made two dressing areas.

Each day, they practiced every move. The singers learned to follow Harry's voice. He even showed a few how to put in a little harmony. Janet still refused to take part in any of the planning or practice, and everyone left her alone. When they were singing, though, Janet hummed the harmony as she pretended to study at her desk.

Izzy and Dell helped Horace with his Santa costume. Izzy found one of Bud's old red bathrobes, which was big enough to cover the sofa pillow to which she had sewn strings. Since the poem said he was covered with ashes and soot, they took some ashes from the stove and a little soot and smeared it over the 'round little belly'. A wide, black belt and Jack's red stocking cap topped off the costume.

For the finishing touch, they planned to paste wads of cotton, saved from the tops of medicine bottles, on his face for a beard. Ma had a whole jar full of cotton she had saved over the years.

On the big day they washed the blackboard before going home and Jack drew a snow-covered Christmas tree.

Everyone pasted his or her paper ornaments on it. Orville reached up to the top and pasted on a shiny star covered with foil gum wrappers.

It was the Friday before vacation started, and they all headed home, hollering and laughing. Izzy knew they were ready for that evening.

# Chapter 19

The four kerosene lamps in their brackets on the walls between the windows provided a dim, warm glow in the tiny schoolroom. Miss Webb stayed at school that afternoon and kept the fire burning, so a warm classroom greeted the students and their guests that evening.

When Pa and Bud brought in the gasoline lantern and the mantle lamp, everything was bright. The closed curtains hid the stage and dressing areas.

"Everything should go perfectly," Izzy said to herself. *We planned everything, and we practiced it all many times.* When she came in, she noticed Janet sitting with her mother and father and her big sister at the side of the room near the back.

Mike arrived and went straight to Izzy. He handed her the Bible and a sheet of paper that said "I can't talk. I choked on a piece of meat and lost my voice."

"Oh no!" Izzy looked around wondered what to do. "I can read the passages that are marked in the Bible, but I'm the producer and need to help Dell with the costumes and the stage props; and I have to point the flashlight for the spotlight," she told Mike. "Well, at least you can handle the flashlight."

She saw Janet out the corner of her eye. *I wonder if she would read. Well, all she can do is say no.*

"Janet, Mike has lost his voice. Can you read the Bible stories in his place?"

"Of course I can. But you'll have to say please before I will."

"Please, pretty please. The passages are all marked." She handed the Bible to Janet.

"Oh, I don't need that. I know all those lines by heart. But maybe you could hold the flashlight on my face instead of on the Bible, sort of like a spotlight. I won't need it on the page like Mike did." Janet sounded a bit smug, but this was no time to create a scene.

"Talk to Mike. He'll be in charge of the flashlight." Izzy quietly sighed in relief.

All the students, except Janet, stood in three rows in front of the curtain. Orville welcomed the audience. Harry stood in front of the students and blew on his little tin pitch pipe, just like his director at church did. Everyone started on the same note.

'We Wish You a Merry Christmas' filled the room.

When the clapping stopped, the students went behind the curtains. Izzy turned off the gasoline lamp and lantern. The room became dim again.

As the curtain opened, Dell and Jim lay on the floor, covered with a quilt. They faced the blackboard at the back of the stage area under the Christmas tree. Jim rolled over, propped himself up on one elbow, and started to recite the poem, while Mike turned Pa's big flashlight on him.

"It was the night before Christmas and all through the house…"

"Louder," Izzy whispered from behind the curtain.

"Not a creature was stirring, not even a mouse," he hollered.

"When out on the lawn, there arose such a clatter . . ."

Dead silence.

"Hey guys, clatter." Izzy whispered loud enough for everyone in the room to hear.

Orville and Jack were supposed to make some noise. Finally, they banged on the stove with some firewood, until Izzy signaled them to stop.

Mike shined the light beam to where Horace was crawling out of the cardboard fireplace, dragging a loaded gunnysack. Everyone clapped. Horace made a convincing miniature Santa.

"He spoke not a word but went straight to his work." Horace reached into the sack for wrapped boxes and some apples to put in the stockings hanging from the cardboard mantle. When he turned with a jerk, he picked up the bottom of the sack and accidentally dumped the whole contents on the floor. As he reached to grab the sack, he knocked his glasses off, and they went skidding across the floor.

Jim did the only thing that any well-mannered boy would do. He hopped up and collected the crumpled newspapers that made the bag look full and stuffed them back, while Santa felt around until he found his glasses. Mike obligingly put the light on the floor to help him.

Horace crawled back into the fireplace. "But I heard him exclaim as he drove out of sight." Jim finished the poem, as Horace yelled from behind the curtain: "Merry Christmas to all, and to all a good night." He forgot to lower his voice, but the audience clapped and clapped. Izzy and Jack closed the curtains, but the clapping continued so long that Izzy told Horace, Jim, and Dell to come back for a curtain call. Dell hadn't even rolled over during the poem, and no one had noticed her. The audience laughed when they saw her, as the makeshift curtain closed.

Now it was time for the main event. Dell and Izzy worked behind the dressing area curtains, getting everyone into their costumes. Jack and Orville removed the fireplace and put the manger in its place. Janet stood in front of the curtain, on one side, and started to recite the Christmas story. Her voice was loud and clear.

Mike held the bright, narrow beam of the flashlight on Janet's face just as she had requested. The bright light made Janet close her eyes, but she still spoke up. At first, she sounded a little timid, but as her eyes adjusted to the light, she spoke louder.

"And it came to pass in those days, there went out a decree from Caesar Augustus, that all the world should be taxed. And Joseph went from Galilee, out of the city of Nazareth, into Judea, unto the city of David, which is called Bethlehem."

Behind the curtain the choir sang,"Oh Little Town of Bethlehem."

Mike turned the flashlight off. Janet whispered, "Leave it off."

When the curtain opened, Joseph and Mary walked slowly across the stage. Joseph pulled Jack's cardboard donkey behind him. The wide beam of the flashlight made a circle of light around Joseph and Mary as they slowly walked across the stage. Joe knocked on the frame of the blackboard.

Jack, dressed in his father's long nightshirt, came from behind the dressing area curtain and shook his head, then pointed to the other end of the stage, to the cardboard manger, full of hay.

Irene walked slowly. She held her arm under the bulge in her oversized blue dress, which belonged to Dell. She wore a light blue scarf on her head. Joseph took a pitchfork and moved some hay from the manger to the floor and put his coat over it. Mary lay down with her back to the audience.

"And so it was, that, while they were there, the days were accomplished that she should be delivered. And she brought forth her firstborn son and wrapped him in swaddling cloths and laid him in a manger, because there was no room for them in the inn." Joe reached down and took the wrapped doll that Irene had taken out from under the dress, and he put it in the manger.

The choir sang, "Away in a manger, no crib for a bed, the little Lord Jesus lay down his sweet head."

Still in the darkness, Janet continued from memory, "And there were in the same country, shepherds abiding in the field, keeping watch over their flock by night." Some of the smaller boys came from behind the curtain next to the right wall, carrying broom handles with cardboard crooks nailed at the top. The big flashlight shined in their faces, and they held their hands up to protect their eyes.

The choir sang "While shepherds watched their flocks by night."

"And the Angel of the Lord came upon them, and the glory of the Lord shone round about them: and they were sore afraid," Janet recited. "Fear not, for unto you is born this day, in the city of David, a savior which is Christ the Lord."

Mike put the spotlight on Harry, who popped up above the curtain while he sang in a clear soprano voice "For unto you a child is born." He stood on a chair on the teacher's desk.

"And suddenly there was with the angel, a multitude of the heavenly host, praising God and singing 'Glory to God in the highest, and peace, good will toward men,'" Janet continued.

All the little girl angels crawled out from under the curtain of the dressing area. The circle of light moved to them. Marie got her wings caught on the sheet, and Maggie called to Harry, still on his high perch, to wait while she untangled her sister. The audience snickered and tried hard not to laugh.

After the angels were in their place, Harry led them in "Hark! The Herald Angels Sing."

The angels crawled back under the curtain and the light shined back on the shepherds.

"As the angels were gone away from them into heaven, the shepherds said one to another, 'Let us now go even unto Bethlehem and see this thing which is come to pass, which the Lord hath made known unto us.'"

The shepherds walked into the stage area where Mary sat beside the manger. She had her hand in the manger and was humming to her baby, and Joseph stood beside his cardboard donkey, smiling. The shepherd looked at the baby and shook hands with Joseph. The flashlight turned off.

Janet continued, "Now, when Jesus was born in Bethlehem of Judea in the days of Herod the king, behold there came wise men from the east."

Mike spotted his flashlight by the left ceiling, over where Orville, Jack, and Jim came from behind the curtains. Each led a cardboard camel.

Harry, Dell and Izzy sang from behind the curtain: "We Three Kings of Orient Are…"

The little procession came down the side aisle, past the windows toward the back of the room, as the spot of light on the ceiling led them. When they got to the back, people on folding chairs filled the space, and they couldn't get to the middle aisle as they had practiced many times. After a little confusion, they parked their camels against the wall, turned around and walked back up the outside aisle, but the star on the ceiling came across the ceiling and up the middle aisle.

When they reached the stage area, the wide beam showed the kings presenting their gifts as they knelt by the manger.

Everyone in the room breathed a big sigh of relief when the curtains closed to a long and loud applause.

Bud and Pa relit the gasoline lamp and lantern.

When the curtain opened again, the complete school, still in their costume and including Janet gathered on the stage and sang "Silent Night." The audience sang with them.

# Chapter 20

Orville came from the back row and made an announcement. "We have all voted not to exchange gifts this year. Instead, we voted to take the money we would have spent on each other, along with the Halloween money, and send it to Chicago for the little kids who live in cardboard boxes under the bridges."

The audience cheered. Mr. O'Malley even passed his hat to make the gift larger.

"If there weren't supposed to be any gifts, what is that under the Christmas tree?" someone asked. They all turned around and saw a small stack of long, narrow boxes, wrapped in Christmas paper.

Orville picked up a package, read the label. It said, "Irene Gruder." Irene tore the paper off. She held up six new pink pencils.

"They've even got my name printed on them," she shouted.

Orville read off more names. Everyone received six pencils in different colors. Dell looked at the label. "Hey everyone, they're from Miss Webb. She must have snuck them in while we were singing."

Orville read Horace's name, but he was nowhere around. "He must have had to go to the can. I'll give him his when he gets back." Everyone had regular pencils with their names on them except Jack. He had a very large box of crayons.

Izzy and Dell started putting cookies on little paper plates that Miss Webb had donated. Orville and Mike brought in the ice cream freezers from outside and brushed the salty ice away from the inner cans. They opened the cans and put homemade ice cream on the plates. Mike's voice seemed completely recovered, as he chattered away. Irene, Jim and Jack passed the goodies to the guests and to the little kids who ran around on the stage, inspecting the fireplace, the cardboard animals, and the crib.

Jingle bells rang outside. Then, Horace, still dressed as Santa, burst through the door, followed by Mr. Turner dragging a heavy-looking gunnysack. "Hey, everyone," Horace shouted.

"Santa Claus didn't go to Florida. He moved to Wisconsin and became Mr. Turner."

He opened the sack and, like a real Santa, he handed toys to each of the kids. The twins and the smaller girls each got a Raggedy Ann doll. The smaller boys got toy trucks or tractors made from wood, while the older boys got toy wooden airplanes with rubber band motors. The older girls each received a hand carved animal made from black walnut wood. Izzy got a neat squirrel, six inches tall, holding a walnut in its paws. Miss Webb even held up a bright yellow roadster, carved out of maple.

Everyone in the room cheered. Mr. Turner and Horace's granny had made a special Christmas for Horace and the kids at Crabapple Creek School.

# Chapter 21

Christmas vacation was over, and 1932 arrived.

Izzy opened her eyes. A fluffy feather bed between the mattress and the fuzzy cotton blankets, used instead of sheets, nestled around her curled-up body. Two or three comforters on top kept out the wind that was whistling around the corner of the house and coming through the cracks between the windows and their frames. She wanted to stay in bed all day. She heard the 'putt-putt-putt' of the milking machine starting up in the barn and smelled bacon coming from the kitchen.

*I wish I could go to Florida with Horace's old Santa.*

"Izzy, time to get up." Ma's voice was cheerful, but Izzy knew that even a cheerful Ma meant what she said.

She reached for her clothes and dragged them under the covers to get them warm and then put them on before she jumped out of the bed.

"Snow and windy conditions are predicted for late today and tonight in southern Wisconsin," the weatherman on the radio in the living room announced. Izzy thought the man's voice was much too cheerful for such gloomy news.

The kerosene lamp in the kitchen flickered and smoked the glass chimney, as wind crept through the windows. The gasoline lamp had lost it fragile mantles from its trip to school, and they had not been replaced. "Today would be a good day for me to stay home and help you. What are you planning to do today?" Izzy asked, hoping to avoid the half-mile trek to school in the cold wind and through the few inches of snow on the ground.

"Oh come on, Izzy. You're going to school just like always. A little old wind never kept us home from school when I was a girl." Ma covered a large bowl of bread dough with a wet towel and placed it on top of the warming oven to rise.

Izzy thought of the smell of bread baking later in the morning but knew it wouldn't do a bit of good to beg to stay home.

After breakfast, she hurried to finish her chores. She pumped water from the cistern and filled the reservoir at the back of the stove. It would provide warm water for washing dishes and hands all day. She put on her coat to empty the slop jars outside and carry wood from the woodshed to fill the wood box.

When she came in from the woodshed with the wood, she took off her coat and put on an extra sweater. "Ma, can I have an old pair of Pa's socks with holes in them? I want to put them over my shoes inside my overshoes."

"Well, okay, but I think you are making too big a deal over a little old snow," Ma replied.

Izzy tied her scarf around her stocking cap and over her mouth. She put a pair of mittens over her gloves. She did not wait for the Gruder family. She knew they didn't like school enough to walk two miles on a day like this. She leaned into the cold wind. Her fingers tingled under her mittens from the cold, but her feet felt okay because of the extra layer of sock. The scarf around her mouth soon become wet from her breath and then froze. Icicles hung from her chin.

When she went into the schoolhouse, the stove gave off heat, but the wood box was almost empty. Miss Webb looked up from where she was writing on the blackboard. "I came early and started the fire because it's Jack's week to build it, and it's Adele's week to carry in wood. I don't think the Gruders will be here today. Will you please bring in some wood, Isabelle?"

All morning, the wind blew harder and harder from the northwest. It was at least three hundred to Lake Superior. The radio man said the wind came from Canada. He called it the "lake effect." It whistled around the corners of the building and rattled the windows. By first recess, a light snow was falling. *It wasn't supposed to snow until tonight,* Izzy thought. Snow piled up on the windowsills, where it blew in around the edges.

At recess Miss Webb asked Izzy and Janet to take used paper from the wastebasket and try to plug the cracks between the windows and the frames. That kept out the snow, but the cold glass and the whistling wind didn't make it seem any warmer. Everyone kept their sweaters on, but the teacher insisted they leave their coats hanging on the hooks in the back. "You'll freeze when you go out if you wear your coats in here."

By noon, the snow was coming down so thick; the woodshed and the outhouses disappeared from sight. Orville lit the kerosene lamps. They didn't help much. All the students' parents except the Gruders' had made them come to school that day.

The students sat on the floor around the stove to eat their dinners. They dragged Jack's cardboard fireplace, manger, camels, sheep, and donkey from behind the book cupboard and used them to sit on because the floor was as cold as the windows. Nobody was very hungry, so there was partly eaten food tossed back in their pails.

Miss Webb looked out the window and said they would just skip the noon hour and second recess so they could go home early. They all liked that idea. By one o'clock, she looked again and said everyone would be safer if they stayed in the building, even if the storm lasted all night.

By two o'clock, the wood box was almost empty. The snow came down so thick, and the wind blew so hard, nobody wanted to get any more.

"We won't even be able to find the woodshed," Mike grumbled.

"Would you rather freeze to death in here, or should we bundle up and go try?" Izzy asked no one in particular. "We can hold hands until we find the woodshed and stand close to each other with our backs to the wind and pass the wood to the nearest window on the east side of the building away from the wind."

A big argument followed. Finally, everyone agreed to try the human chain idea, if Izzy went first. "No, I'll go first," Miss Webb volunteered. She had unintentionally outwitted them all because she stood in the shed out of the wind, picking up pieces of wood and passing them on, one at a time.

They passed each piece to the first window, which was open just enough for Orville to fit in a single piece. The little kids inside passed each piece to the wood box. The box filled in a hurry. They stacked more wood in the corner. Everyone worked so hard that they felt almost warm when they closed the window.

All that work had made everyone hungry. Some wanted to eat anything that was left over in their dinner pails. Miss Webb said, "No. It's going to be a long night. We'll take turns dipping new snow by the door and heating it on the stove."

"Why can't we just eat the snow?" Jim wanted to know.

"That will just make you colder, dummy," Orville told him.

The kerosene in the lamps looked to be about used up, so all but one was blown out, to save the rest for the night. They all agreed: one lamp at a time would be better than none. They hoped their parents would know that the teacher had enough sense not to make them go home in snow so thick and wind so strong that they would get lost.

The teacher gave up trying to do lessons at about two o'clock and had all the students gather in front of the stove. The stove door was left open to let out more heat, and enough light from the fire made it possible to read. The older students took turns reading out loud from the storybooks in the book cupboard.

"This is just like the olden days when all the people had were fireplaces," Janet remarked. They all sat close together and shared each other's warmth. By four, no light came through the windows. Everyone looked in his or her dinner pail. They put all the leftover food into some water made from the melted snow and set it on the stove. When it was hot enough, everyone had a tin cup full of hot soup. They all agreed that it tasted funny but helped make them feel full. Mike and Orville put on their coats and brought in another pail of snow to melt, so they could have some water to drink.

*I wonder if Pa and Ma are okay. Will Pa get lost trying to get to the barn to feed and milk the cows? Will Bud stay in town? Did the high school send the students home early?*

Some of the little kids had already fallen asleep on the cardboard mats. Janet and Izzy covered them up with their coats. They stacked books around the little circle of humanity to cut down on the draft. The older students started telling stories.

They heard the big eight-sided clock over the blackboard, ticking away. Mixed with the sound of the storm, it made everyone sleepy. The one lamp grew dim and flickered out, so Orville lit another. Miss Webb said everyone should lie close together, and she covered them up with their coats. She appointed Izzy and Janet to stay awake for a couple hours to keep the fire going. At midnight, they could wake up Orville and Mike to take over. She volunteered to finish up the night by herself.

# Chapter 22

Izzy opened her eyes. Dim light crept though the windows. Frost covered the glass in a riot of white, tropical-looking foliage. Miss Webb sat at her desk in her coat, sound asleep. When Izzy stirred, the teacher opened her eyes.

Izzy needed to go to the outhouse in the worst way. The clock sounded louder than ever, and the wind had died down. She roused herself and went to the east window. By blowing on the glass, she melted a hole in the frost that was big enough to look through. She saw solid snow. She blinked her eyes in disbelief. The wall of snow was above the eaves of the tiny schoolhouse, two feet away from the building. A narrow tunnel led to the back of the building.

Miss Webb put more wood on the fire and closed the stove door. Izzy whispered to the teacher, who nodded. When Izzy came back inside, the teacher asked her to take over while she went outside. Now, everyone was stirring. When Izzy told them the storm was over and the routes to the outhouses were clear, they all quickly put on their coats and rushed outside.

Before long, several fathers showed up with their teams and bobsleds. The sled boxes contained straw and blankets to cover the children and take them home to a hot breakfast.

Miss Webb's yellow car was completely buried in snow.

"You can come home with me. We'll dig your car out later," Janet's father told her. "There will be no school today," he told the students. Because he was chairman of the school board, he had the authority to cancel school.

"I'll call the Gruders from your place," Miss Webb said.

The bright sun felt wonderful. Izzy wrapped the heavy blanket over her head and all the way to her feet as she sat on the spring seat beside Pa. The horses were lively as they trotted toward home with their blankets secure over the harness.

They went around a big snowdrift by the lilac bushes. Pa had cut the barbed wire fence earlier to get to the school.

"How did you find the barn to take care of the animals yesterday?" she asked.

"Well, about noon, I heard a warning on the radio that we might experience a whiteout, so I went to the barn and tied the trip rope from the hay fork onto the barn door and stretched it to the back steps of the porch. Sure glad I did.

I lit the gasoline lantern, but it only made the snow seem whiter. Great help in the barn, though."

Ma had breakfast ready when they got home. Izzy couldn't drink coffee, because she was too young, but she loved the smell of it brewing, and the bacon smelled wonderful. Ma even made a special treat for her—hot cocoa.

"Where's Bud?" Izzy asked.

"He stayed in town with a friend," Pa told her. "I could sure use his help shoveling out some paths."

Even though Mr. Andrews had told them that they had the day off, Izzy was wide-awake. "Tell us about some of the winters you had in the olden days," she begged her parents.

"Well, there was the time when I was courting your ma, and the cutter tipped over," Pa said.

"Yes, you turned the corner too fast, and that old sleigh just flipped on its side and threw me clean out, headfirst, into the snow-bank, and you ran after the horses instead of helping me." Ma shook her fist at Pa, but she was laughing.

"Well, if I hadn't, we'd have had to walk home." Everyone laughed.


The next morning, Pa put the scoop shovel over his shoulder and walked to school with Izzy. They walked in the field around the big snowdrift in the road caused by the lilac bushes. Several tracks showed where other sleds had been. For a while, those tracks would be the road.

Pa was joined by Mr. Andrews and Mr. O'Malley. By first recess, Miss Webb's Chevy was freed from the huge drift by the schoolhouse.

Before starting classes, Miss Webb asked the students what they had learned from the big storm. Mike said he'd never seen a snowdrift so high that it covered a whole car. Orville said he learned that if they all worked together, they could do the impossible, like filling the wood box when they couldn't even see the wood. "Hey, it was even fun, and we almost kept warm all night too."

Janet asked the teacher if she had learned anything.

"Yes, I did. I learned what a great bunch of students I have. I'm proud of how each of you pitched in to help us survive. Now, it's time to get back to our regular lessons."

# Chapter 23

"Seventh and eighth grade civics," Miss Webb announced. Orville, Izzy, and Mike moved to the recitation bench.

"Have you all read the assignment?" Miss Webb asked. All three heads nodded.

"What is the lesson about, Orville?" Orv pushed some hair out of his eyes and cleared his throat.

"It's about electing the president."

"Can you briefly tell us how it's done?" Miss Webb sat on her chair, which she had placed in front of the recitation bench.

"Well, every state votes for something called electors, who get together and pick who they want to be the president. Then, the electors send their choices to Washington." Orv looked at Mike and Izzy with a trace of a smirk, as if to say, "See, I actually did read the lesson."

"That seems like a dumb way to elect anyone. Why don't they just count all the votes and make the winner the president like we do?" Mike asked. Izzy figured that he hadn't read the lesson, but probably hoped, by speaking up, that Miss Webb wouldn't know the difference.

"Can anyone think of a reason why it is the way it is?" the teacher asked.

Izzy raised her hand. "The Constitution was written one hundred fifty years ago. They didn't have radios or railroads, and even newspapers didn't get to everyone, so the people didn't know who would be a good president or a bad president. When the Continental Congress was trying to form the new government, they thought if the people picked a trusted neighbor, the men from each state could get together somewhere central like say Philadelphia or Annapolis, to discuss the problems of running the country. That way, they could get to know different people in their groups and make good choices."

Mike stuck his tongue out at Izzy when the teacher had her head turned. Izzy gave him an elbow in the ribs.

"Very good. Now, can anyone tell us how a president can be removed from office?"

"He can be impeached," Mike volunteered. "My old man says they should impeach Mr. Hoover, 'cause he caused this Depression."

"He's your father, Michael, not your old man," The teacher corrected him.

Izzy defended the president. "My father says it isn't Mr. Hoover's fault. He says all the greedy people who tried to get rich quick and borrowed money to buy stock caused it. They couldn't cover their losses when the market crashed."

"Well, he ought to be impeached," Mike insisted.

"The only reason for impeaching a public officer is if he commits a crime. Mr. Hoover hasn't committed any crime, so there's no reason to impeach him," Izzy said, "So there."

Miss Webb asked Orville what he thought.

"Ghee whiz, I don't know. The country is sure in a mess right now, what with everyone except the farmers out of work and all, but I don't have any idea how it happened or what to do about it. The vice president probably couldn't do any better. I just don't know." Orville wrinkled his brow and frowned.

# Chapter 24

Winter gave way to spring. The snow melted, and the road turned from snow to mud.

On their way to school, Jack and Izzy walked on the brown grass in the middle of the road, between the muddy ruts. When they passed the lilac bushes, they couldn't see Miss Webb's yellow roadster because a big black Buick stood in the way, beside it.

"I wonder whose car that it is." Izzy loved cars, all kinds of cars, and she knew the make and model of every car on the road.

"It's a big one, all right. No wonder they need chains to get through all this mud." Jack looked at the chains wrapped around the hind wheels.

When they entered the schoolhouse, a pretty young lady with short, curly, brown hair and bright red lipstick sat at the teacher's desk. As soon as everyone settled down after the bell, Miss Webb introduced the new person. "This is Miss Helen Jordon. Miss Jordon is a student teacher at the County Normal School. She will be observing and helping me for a couple weeks to get experience."

Izzy pulled her own streaky braids as she admired the stranger's short, curly hair, and she bit her lips so they would turn a little red. The twins stared in open admiration, and Mike and Orville's eyes had a certain sparkle.

Next morning, Mike arrived early and carried the young intern's books. Orville took his red handkerchief out of his pocket and wiped the mud off the yellow isinglass window in the back of the car. Izzy noticed this unusual behavior and wondered if they were planning some sort of mischief.

The next Monday, Miss Webb sneezed every few minutes and constantly wiped her nose. Tuesday morning, no yellow roadster sat at the side of the building. "Miss Webb is sick," Miss Jordon told the students. "Mr. Andrews has asked me to carry on for the week."

In late March, most of the snow had melted. Crabapple Creek, behind the wire fence of the school yard, flowed over its banks. The wind blew in gusts. At the noon recess, everybody stayed inside and ate their dinner.

Mike and Orville went outside for ten or fifteen minutes, while everyone else played twenty questions. That afternoon, as lessons droned on, Izzy had a funny feeling and decided to check it out. She raised her hand to go to the outhouse. When she rounded the corner of the schoolhouse, she saw smoke coming from the door of the woodshed. She ran and looked inside. A good-sized fire burned in the stored wood. Flames reached to the roof.

"Don't panic," Izzy told herself as she dashed toward the tiny schoolhouse.

*Slow down; don't run.* She walked up to the new teacher and whispered in her ear. The teacher turned white and fainted. The thump on the floor made everyone look up. Izzy's mouth fell open as she looked at the fallen teacher. She looked for Orville to see if he showed any sign of taking charge, but he just sat at his desk with his eyes popping out.

*Keep your voice calm.* Izzy looked around the room.

"Listen up, everyone. We have a problem. The woodshed is on fire, and the wind is blowing right toward the schoolhouse. The teacher isn't going to be much help, so we have to take charge," she told the room full of students as calmly as possible.

# Chapter 25

The twins, Maggie and Marie, started to cry. Izzy barked at them. "Stop that right now. You two, go grab the bell rope and start ringing the bell, and don't stop until I tell you to." They stopped crying, ran, and grabbed the rope.

"Now, Janet, you throw some water on the teacher and get her out of here. Mike, find her keys and move her car away from the buildings. We don't need the gas tank to blow up." Izzy felt more confident now, as she took a deep breath and gave orders.

"The rest of you, dump your dinner pails and make a line from the fence to the back of the schoolhouse. Jack, you climb over the fence and dip water out of the creek for the kids to pass to Orv and Dell. Orv and Dell, you throw water on the back wall of the building so it won't catch on fire." Dell was big and strong. Orville was six feet tall and could reach almost to the eaves of the tiny building.

Everyone rushed to do as she told them.

When she left the building and looked up, embers were blowing onto the roof. "Oh ghee, I forgot all about the roof." Izzy rushed back into the building, took her coat, and plunged it into the water cooler. She ran out to the porch and undid the flag rope. The flag had not been raised that day because of the wind. She snapped a buckle into a buttonhole of her coat.

*I sure hope this rope doesn't pull the pulley off the top and let me fall,* she thought as she tried to climb it to the roof. In her haste, she forgot she needed to hold onto both the up and down rope. She saw the coat head up while she still stood on the steps. *Well, dummy, you have to hang onto both ropes if you want to get on the roof.* After several tries, she managed to walk up the clapboard wall, hand over hand, by pulling on the ropes.

The bell kept ringing, as she pulled up her wet coat. When she tried to walk on the steep roof, her smooth shoes slipped, and she fell on her knees. "Woops, I almost fell off." She dug her fingernails into the rough shingles and felt slivers but ignored them.

More embers fell on the roof. Several wooden shingles started to burn.

Izzy crawled on her hands and knees to each flame and beat it out with her wet coat. Cars and trucks arrived from all directions. Men and women with pails and kettles took over the 'bucket brigade', and the woodshed fire was soon under control.

Janet's father brought a ladder and joined Izzy on the roof. Embers no longer filled the air. Her knees bled through her torn stockings, and her ripped dress showed her underwear.

"How did you get up here?" he asked.

"I climbed up the flag rope." Izzy shivered from excitement and relief that the crisis seemed under control and that she no longer needed to be in charge.

For the first time, she realized that she was cold. Mr. Andrews took off his jacket and wrapped it around her. Her dirty, wet coat lay in a black heap on the roof. He kicked it to the ground.

The bell still rang when Izzy climbed down the ladder. "You can quit ringing it now," she told the frightened twins. "You did a great job."

"Looks like everyone did a great job," Mr. Andrews told the group of adults and students gathered around the smoldering woodshed. Mothers wrapped their coats about the little ones and held them close to get them warm.

"How did the fire get started?" Mr. Andrews asked.

"Maybe someone was smoking in the woodshed," Dell suggested.

Mr. Andrews nodded his head. "That sounds reasonable. Maybe we need to have a pocket inspection." Orville then blurted out that he and Mike might have smoked a butt or two, but he swore up and down that they had put them out.

The boys' fathers, Mr. Brown and Mr. O'Malley, spoke to each other at one side. Then, Mr. O'Malley came forward. "Since our boys probably caused the fire, we'll rebuild the woodshed and replace the wood. I have some boards that were left when I tore down a shed, and Brown will cut some poles from his woods. You can be sure, the boys will be punished." Izzy almost felt sorry for them.

# Chapter 26

The next morning, everyone went to school as usual. A pile of firewood was dumped near the door. Izzy wore her forbidden overalls because her only dress was now just a rag. She noticed that Orville and Mike no longer plopped into their seats, as they usually did, but sat down very carefully.

Outside, a commotion made everyone look around. Miss Webb, back from her illness, sent Janet out to see what was going on. Mike's and Orville's fathers had driven into the driveway with their wagons loaded with poles, boards, and tools. Mike's father shouted through the door. "Get out here, you two. If you think you're men enough to smoke, you're men enough to help build this here woodshed." Miss Webb did not stop them.

At noon, everyone went out to watch. Mr. Brown had dug five holes in the ground and placed upright poles for the four corners and the doorway, while Mike and Orville unloaded the boards that Mr. O'Malley measured and sawed. When the poles were set in the ground, the boys started nailing the boards to the two-by-sixes spiked to the top and bottom of the upright poles. Mike tried to hit a nail and missed it, hitting his thumb. He hollered a bad word and jumped around with his thumb in his mouth.

"That'll learn ya to be sure your butt is out before ya throw it where it'll start a fire," his father growled at him.

Orville reached over his head to nail the boards at the top. When his hammer hit a nail on its edge, it bent. He turned the hammer over, pulled the nail out with the claws and threw it on the ground.

"Hey, boy," his father barked. "Pick that up and straighten it. Them there nails cost money, ya know."

The rest of the students sat in a half-circle on their dinner pails to stay off the cold, wet ground. They enjoyed watching the big guys work.

"I thought Orv would be better with a hammer than that," Dell commented. "He always shows off with it when he's presiding over a meeting."

"Some president—presidents are supposed to be leaders," Janet added. "Maybe he should be impeached. After all, what he and Mike did could be called a crime."

"Mike's the vice-president now; that would make him president," Jack warned.

"Impeach both of them," Jim suggested. Izzy guessed that they had been listening to the seventh and eighth grade civics class.

By Friday, the woodshed was finished. Orville and Mike were back in the classroom for the meeting.

"The weekly meeting of The Friday Afternoon Society will come to order." Orville sat in the teacher's chair. Izzy, as secretary/treasurer, sat to the left of him on one of the visitors' chairs. She wore a new blue dress with a sailor's collar that Ma had made from new cloth. Ma had even used a store-bought pattern. Two blue matching bows perched at the ends of her braids. Miss Webb sat at the back of the room. The young intern had not returned.

After the routine business of reading the minutes and electing next week's duty officers was completed, the president called for new business.

Janet jumped up. "Mr. President, I move we impeach the president and the vice president."

"You can't do that, because I resign." Orville's new manly voice squeaked the last three words. He picked up his hammer and stormed out the door.

"Me too," Mike announced, as he followed behind Orville.

The whole school watched them go. Izzy looked at Miss Webb, who sat at the dictionary table at the back. She didn't look up, as she pretended to correct papers.

Izzy couldn't rap the hammer because Orville had taken it, so she made a fist and knocked on the desk. "I guess I'm the only officer left, so I'll have to take over. Nominations are now open for the position of president."

Everyone in the room jumped up and called to be recognized. Izzy called on Janet to speak.

Janet jumped to her feet. "I nominate Isabelle Norton."

Everyone else stood up and cheered, yelling, "I second the nomination." Even Miss Webb clapped. *She must have been listening all along.*

"It seems to be unanimous," the new president remarked.

"If there is no further business, The Friday Afternoon Society of Crabapple Creek School is adjourned."

"Yippee!" Jack jumped two feet off the ground and kicked his heels together as soon as they went past the lilac bushes that hid them from the school.

"What are you so happy about?" Izzy asked.

"That ornery old Orv and mean old Mike got just what they deserved."

Izzy's face still glowed with excitement. "Well, Ghee!" She wanted to sound calm about the whole thing but had a hard time not showing how excited she felt. "It was either me or Janet, and she couldn't very well nominate herself. Besides, it's only for two months. School will be out in May, and next year, we'll start all over." "What're you going to do first?" Dell asked. Dell could quit school the next month, because the law no longer required her to attend.

"I don't know. I've only been president ten minutes. I know what I'd like to do. I'd like to get rid of electing all those duty officers every week. It seems like I carry water or fill the wood box every other week."

"Great idea, Izzy," Kitty, a third grader, agreed.

"I think we should just vote for Orv and Mike to do all those boring duties all the time," Irene declared.


"Ma! Ma! Guess what?" Izzy shouted, as she dashed into the kitchen.

"Good Lord, what now?"

"The whole school elected me president."

"Oh my, you gave me such a scare, coming in all excited that way. I thought something awful must have happened again." Ma turned away from the hot cook stove and wiped her forehead with her apron.

"Janet moved to impeach Orville, and the big boob resigned. Then he and Mike ran away. She nominated me, and the whole school cheered."

"That's wonderful. Pa and I are so proud of you, how you took charge when the woodshed burned, and you organized everyone to save the schoolhouse. But being president is a big responsibility. You better make sure you don't mess up."

# Chapter 27

"Crabapple Creek Friday Afternoon Society will come to order." Her voice could barely be heard. *Louder, Izzy,* she told herself. Butterflies danced a polka in her stomach as she lightly tapped the teacher's desk with her knuckles for her first meeting as president.

"We can't start yet. Orv ain't back from the can," Mike said. "I'll go get him." He jumped up and hurried out the door.

Five minutes passed. The kids began to murmur with little conversations. No Orville or Mike showed up. "Jack, will you go see what the problem is?" Izzy asked.

"They're both gone. Their dinner pails are gone too. I guess they skipped out," Jack said when he returned.

"Well, we'll just have to start without them." *Thank you, Lord,* she silently prayed.

"The first order of business is to elect a new vice president and a secretary/treasurer."

"Madam President." Janet Andrews stood up, her long blond curls gleaming in the afternoon sun that was coming though the window.

"Miss Andrews."

"I nominate Miss Adele Gruder for vice president."

Dell had only reached sixth grade. "Oh no, you don't. I ain't got but two more weeks before I'm sixteen, and I won't have to come to school no more," Dell almost shouted.

Miss Webb sitting at the back of the room, closed her eyes, and shook her head.

Jack jumped to his feet. "I nominate Janet Andrews."

"Oh no, you don't." Janet echoed Dell's remark. "I don't want to be vice president; I want to be secretary/treasurer."

"Nomination declined," Izzy announced. "Are there any other nominations for vice president?"

Harry stood up. "I nominate Jim Marshall."

Finally, Jim was elected vice president, and Janet got her wish to be secretary/treasurer.

"We will now have the election of duty officers for next week. Water carriers," Izzy announced.

"I nominate Mike and Orv," Kitty Gruder announced. The nomination was seconded and passed.

"Fireman." Still cold in March, the elected fireman came to school early every morning for a week to build a fire in the heating stove.

"I nominate Orv." Irene made good on her threat to elect Orv and Mike to all the duties.

"You can't do that. He is already the water carrier," Izzy objected.

"Where is it written that someone can't have two duties?" Irene asked.

"I don't know, but that wouldn't be fair. I don't even know if we've ever had any written rules."

"Well, I second the nomination of Orville Brown for fireman," her sister Kitty said.

When Izzy asked for the vote, every student in the room raised a hand. Izzy looked at Miss Webb, who winked at her but offered no help.

And so it went. Orv or Mike won every duty except sweeping the girl's outhouse.

Izzy felt her face getting hot. *Being president isn't as much fun as I thought it would be.*

"Well, if that's the way you want it. Harry, you go by Orville's place on your way home. You can tell him that he is fireman next week, so he'll get here early to build the fire, and tell him about all the other duties too."

"Oh no, he'd probably punch me in the nose. I don't want to." Harry scuffed his feet and studied a broken shoelace.

"Well, do I see any volunteers?" Not a hand went up.

"Janet, as secretary, will you write the duty winners on the blackboard? And I suggest that everyone wear an extra sweater Monday, just in case Orv decides he doesn't feel like building a fire. I'll call his mother on the phone and tell her about the duty. Oh yes, and everybody better put a jar of water in their dinner pail. Make it a quart jar, so you'll have enough to wash your hands too. That won't leave much room for food, but the guys may decide they don't want to carry the water either."

"Hey, maybe we made a mistake," Jack said. "I know I wouldn't want all those duties the same week." A buzz arose as everyone talked to each other, but nobody asked to be recognized.

Finally, Janet moved that they cancel the first election and start over.

# Chapter 28

The following Friday, Izzy opened the meeting. After completing the routine business she announced, "We're going to have a convention to write some rules for 'The Friday Afternoon Society'. Every two grades will send a delegate. Right now, you can get together and pick someone: first and second graders, third and fourth graders, fifth and sixth graders, and seventh and eighth graders."

The little room buzzed with conversation as different groups started talking to each other. Izzy walked back to talk to Orville and Mike. "Which one of you will represent our group?" she asked.

"I don't give a hoot about your old rules. In two months, I'll graduate," Orv grunted.

"You always seem to know all the answers; I'm just a dumb old farmer, so do whatever you want to. I don't care," Mike growled.

"Okay, okay. I'll represent us, but I don't want to hear either of you whining about what the committee may decide."

Each group announced their delegates.

Horace stood up. "They picked me to do it for first and second grade."

"Third and fourth chose me," Irene said.

"I'll represent fifth and sixth grades," Janet announced

"Over the weekend, the delegates can think about what kind of rules we need, and we'll meet Monday during noon while we eat dinner. The weather isn't fit for us to be outside anyway."

By Monday, the thrill of representing others had worn off. The gloomy April day dulled the enthusiasm of the little group huddled on the recitation bench with their round dinner pails between their knees like milk pails. Izzy sat in the teacher's chair, while Miss Webb ate her dinner at the back.

"I read up on the Constitution," Janet announced. "First, we need a preamble. Then we'll need articles, sections, and amendments. I'm the secretary, so I can be like James Madison and write it."

"That's dumb," Irene objected, wrinkling her nose.

Horace raised his hand. "I know—we can just think up a few rules and Janet can write them in the minutes notebook. Then we'll have written rules."

"Well, that would at least be a start," Izzy agreed. "Janet, take notes please."

"So, what are the problems?" Izzy asked.

"The problem is those dumb duty officers," Irene said. "Everybody knows they're just chores. We all have to do chores at home. Why do we have to do chores at school too?"

"Well, somebody has to do them," Horace spoke up.

"Let the teacher do that stuff. She gets paid," Irene argued.

Izzy disagreed. "That's not fair either. She only gets fifty dollars a month, and she has to teach eight different grades and mark all those papers with that red pencil of hers."

"Well, okay, I guess" Irene said reluctantly. "At our house, the four of us little kids have a chart. Our ma changes it every month so we don't get stuck emptying slop jars all the time."

"That's your first helpful remark, and it even makes sense," Izzy said to Irene. The group nodded agreement. "Do you move to have a chore chart?"

"I guess." Irene grunted.

"All in favor raise your hands." Horace and Irene raised their hands.

"But what about our constitution?" Janet asked, voting no.

"It can wait. We'll start by seeing if the rest of the school approves of the idea of a chore chart. Janet, write a short report of this meeting to read Friday. Now, let's eat." Izzy sighed with relief.

The word about the chore chart spread fast. All week, Izzy overheard different little groups talking about it. Mike grumbled during recess that the whole idea was illegal because the president was a girl, and girls couldn't be president.

"Janet's read up on the Constitution of the United States. Ask her if it says anything there about women not being president," Izzy suggested.

"The Constitution doesn't say anything about women," Janet announced in her 'I-know-it-all' voice.

"Okay, there's your answer," Izzy told Mike. He sneered.

"This isn't the United States. This is Crabapple Creek Friday Afternoon Society, and I was elected president by everyone that was there. You and Orv resigned and ran away, so you don't have anything to complain about."

"That just proves that we need our own constitution," Janet pointed out.

By Friday afternoon, everyone was ready. After Janet read the regular minutes, Izzy called for the committee report.

Janet's report was short and to the point. "The special committee voted two to one, to recommend replacing elected duty officers with a chore chart to be changed every month."

Irene waved her hand. "I move we adopt the recommendation." Horace seconded. "The floor is open for discussion," the president said.

Susan, a second grader, raised her hand. "Does that mean we have to carry water for a whole month at a time?"

"No, dummy," Irene retorted. "Little kids can do stuff like cleaning the erasers, sweeping the outhouses, and emptying the pencil sharpener and wastebasket. The big kids will carry the water and the wood and take care of the stove."

Horace raised his hand. "I think we need two charts: one for us and one for the big kids." The group murmured approval.

Susan added, "Change that to read every week."

"Do I hear a motion to amend the first motion to read 'two chore charts, to be changed every week'?"

Someone uttered, "I so move."

The amendment was seconded and approved.

"Who's going to make the chart, and how can we be sure we don't get stuck with some crappy chore every other week?" Harry asked.

Jack sat at his desk, doodling during the entire discussion. Jim looked over at Jack's drawing—a picture of an American flag on the belfry of a little schoolhouse.

"I know," Jim suggested, "Jack can make a big, round cardboard wheel and draw pictures of all the chores on the outside. He's always drawing anyway. We can put a smaller wheel with everyone's name on the edge and put it over the big wheel. Then we can tack it on the back of the door with a thumbtack in the middle and turn the names every Friday."

"That's a great idea, Jim," Izzy said. "Do you think you can do that, Jack?" Izzy asked.

"Sure, if somebody will give me some cardboard," Jack agreed.

"Hey," Susan interrupted, "What about us little kids? You said we would have two charts."

"Okay, okay. I'll make two charts," Jack agreed.

"Susan, I appoint you and Jim to get with Jack and plan which chores will go on which chart," Izzy said.


Mike stood up. "I move we disband the Friday Afternoon Society." Orville seconded the motion.

A murmur rose throughout the room.

"Okay, is there any discussion?" Izzy said after fumbling with her pencil and scribbling some question marks on her tablet. Half a dozen hands went up.

"Now that there ain't no duty officers to elect, there ain't no sense of having Friday Afternoon Society," Mike said.

Izzy had to think fast. She wanted to keep on being president. "Well in case you missed it, the whole point of the society is to teach us how to run and take part in organized meetings. We use the same rules that they use in Congress."

"Yeah, yeah, yeah," Mike blurted out. "All of us are going to go be congressmen. Maybe I'll even be president. I could do better than that creepy old Hoover guy."

"If you ever are, I'm moving to Canada," Izzy snapped. Several students tittered.

"What good is the old society if we don't elect duty officers anymore?" Orville asked.

Good old Dell came to Izzy's rescue. "Playday is coming up. Izzy's pretty good at organizing. Maybe she can get us better organized, so we can beat those snots from Wilcox School. I might even stay in school another month to be sure."

Horace raised his hand. "Last year for Halloween, we had a program and box supper. That was fun."

Harry raised his hand. "Maybe we can do that again next year. Then we could have other stuff like a barn dance and sell tickets or take a trip somewhere. It could be some place that has a history, like that old house south of here where they hid slaves during the Civil War."

Before long, almost everyone had some suggestions. Some were crazy, and some sounded like fun. Izzy finally cut them off.

"All in favor of disbanding the Friday Afternoon Society raise your hands."

Only Mike and Orville voted *yes*. Everyone else voted *no*. Izzy let out a quiet sigh of relief.

"Starting Monday, we're going to have kittenball practice after supper. Ask your big brothers and sisters to come too. We can have two teams and play some real games instead of work-up."

Horace raised his hand. "What's kittenball?" he asked.

"That's like baseball only with a smaller diamond and a biggest ball. As far as I'm concerned, that old kittenball is just as hard as a baseball, only bigger," Janet told him.

Susan waved her hand. "How about us little kids? We're a part of Playday too, you know."

"I know. I know. We'll help all of you prepare for your events too," Izzy told her. "Janet, you can sew. You make some beanbags for the beanbag toss."

"I can, but I think it would be nice if the honorable president would ask, instead of ordering me," Janet pouted.

"Okay, Miss Andrews," Izzy said with and exaggerated smile, "Will you be so kind as to sew some lovely beanbags for the younger students to use to practice tossing into a special box so they may become good at hitting the target?" A few snickers bounced around the room.

"Orv, do you think you could make the box for the target?" Izzy asked in her normal voice.

"I suppose so," Orville grunted.

"Every recess, we'll practice different events like beanbag toss, running, and the baseball-throw. We'll pick the fastest four for the relay races. First, second, and third graders can be in the baseball throw, the hundred-yard relay race, and beanbag toss. Those events are separate competition just for the little kids," Izzy said.

"Hey, do you think we can really beat that bunch from Wilcox?" Dell sounded excited.

# Chapter 29

Izzy sniffed as she went down the stairs. The smell of bacon and coffee met her nose. But something else didn't smell as good. When she entered the kitchen, Ma was being sick over the garbage pail.

"What's the matter, Ma?"

"I am so sick to my stomach. The smell of bacon never made me sick before," Ma gasped.

Izzy handed her a dipper of water from the well-water pail. "Here, rinse your mouth out, and then go back to bed. I'll finish breakfast."

Pa and Bud came in from doing the milking. "Oh no, not Izzy's cooking again. I think I'm going to be sick," Bud said. "I smell a sick feeling coming on."

"Bud, just be glad Izzy's making breakfast, or you'd be doing it. Now, pick up that garbage pail, and take it outside and dump it." Pa raised his arm as if to swat Bud in the seat of his pants. Bud grabbed the pail and soon returned from his unpleasant duty.

"Bud, you're a pretty good ball player; do you think you could help us get our kittenball team ready for Playday?" Izzy asked, after Pa finished the blessing.

"Maybe," he replied. "What's in it for me?"

"If we could get all the young guys and girls that are past grade school to come down to the school yard after supper every night, we could practice with two actual teams. Maggie O'Malley and Ingrid Andrews might even be there. It would be a chance for you to show them what a big strong athlete you are."

"Is that a promise?" Bud asked.

"No, it is not a promise." Izzy stuck her tongue out at Bud.

On Monday night, about twenty young people showed up at the ball field. Even some of the little kids were there. "First thing we need to do is choose sides," Izzy said. The group made Orville and Izzy opposing captains. Bud tossed the bat in the air, and Izzy caught it. Hand-over-hand, the first fingers to reach the top belonged to Orville. "I pick Mike," he said.

"I'll take Dell," Izzy countered.

Soon, two teams squared off, and everyone had so much fun that they played until they couldn't see the ball in the dark.

"Friday Afternoon Society will come to order."

"Night practice was fun, but we need to get better organized," Izzy announced. "What we need to do is get a permanent captain and pick the players who are best in each position."

"I nominate Orv," Mike said. "He's the best player."

"I nominate Izzy," Dell countered. "She's the best at knowing the rules and figuring out what to do." The vote was a tie. Izzy didn't want to break the tie with her own vote. She went through an elaborate process of counting the hands, to give her time to think of something.

Horace solved the problem. "Maybe we could have co-captains."

Orville grunted, "Okay."

After the meeting, Izzy cornered Orville before he got away and told him they needed to decide who would play where and then have each player get good at playing that position. To her surprise, he agreed.

At practice that evening, they asked each kid to decide where he or she wanted to play, and then they held tryouts. They decided that Mike and Dell would take turns at pitcher and catcher. Orville, because of his long arms and legs, was unanimous choice for first base. Izzy could run the fastest and throw the farthest, so she became the center fielder. Janet ended up in right field because she couldn't do any of those things, but nobody ever hit the ball to right field anyway.

"Friday Afternoon Society will come to order."

"We're getting good at our positions, but what we need is more spirit as a team," Dell declared.

"How do you intend to do that?" Mike sneered.

Horace raised his hand. "In Chicago, everyone cheers for the Cubs or the White Sox. We need to give our team a name."

"I know. I know," Janet shouted. "We're Crabapple Creek. We can be the 'Apple Blossoms.'"

"That's dumb," Mike yelped. "A team name has to sound mean, like Tigers or Pirates."

"Maybe we should name the team Crabs. I've seen pictures of crabs, and they look plenty mean," Irene suggested.

"This is Wisconsin, for Pete's sake. Whoever heard of crabs in Wisconsin?" Izzy asked. "Most people here have never even seen a crab."

"My big brother had something called crabs once," Jack said. "They were some sort of lice. They were small, but they were mean. The whole family got 'em. They bit and itched something awful. He called them cooties."

"That's it. We can be the 'Cooties'," Orville said. "Except for me and Dell, we're small, but we're mean when we play ball."

"Right," Dell agreed. "You can be Papa Louse, and I'll be Mama Louse. We'll bite that Wilcox gang where they can't scratch."

"I think that's terrible," Janet snorted.

Orville moved, and Jim seconded that they name the team "Cooties."

"Motion carried, seventeen to one."

"The Cubs all dress alike, and so do the White Sox," an excited Horace added. "Maybe we can all dress alike."

"Look around, Horace. The guys all dress alike now," Jim said. Horace had gotten new overalls for Christmas instead of those sissy knickers. "All we need to do is get Miss Prissy Janet into a pair of overalls, and we'll have it made. We know that the rest of the girls on the team wear overalls when they're not made to wear a dress."

Janet's face turned bright red. "There is no way that I am going to wear a pair of ragged old overalls. Just because the rest of you girls don't mind looking like scarecrows, doesn't mean I have to."

Izzy frowned. "You'll look out of place, but I guess that's your problem."

Jack waved his hand. "I know. I can draw a picture of a cootie on bibs of the overalls." He held up a piece of paper with a cartoon of a mean looking louse on it."

Izzy liked the idea. "Put the crayon on thick, and then melt the wax in with a hot flatiron. That'll make it permanent."

"That would ruin the ironing board and irons," Dell said.

"Not if you put a piece of paper under and over the picture," Izzy told her.

# Chapter 30

Everyone worked hard at his or her position. The older guys coached them. Dell stayed in school and even tried to study some. "Maybe I'll even know enough to pass. We're mostly reviewing now anyway."

Jack made pictures on all the overalls, and Dell ironed them in. The little kids, who probably weren't going to play ball, even brought an extra pair to have their cootie drawn. Izzy told them that they would be the cheering section. Jack put a cootie on his best pair, just in case Janet relented. Then he put triangles, cut from the sides of a worn-out sheet, on sticks and made banners for the little kids to wave. On the big end was a louse, followed by the word *COOTIES*.

Izzy told the younger students that they were just as important as the players and added that they might even be substitute players.

Finally, the big day arrived. The Norton's one lone rooster, Henry, crowed, and Izzy sprang out of bed. She tiptoed past Ma's bedroom door, but Ma called to her. "I'm so sick, you'll have to get breakfast and fix something for the Playday picnic." Izzy wondered why Ma was sick every morning.

As the bacon sizzled and the coffee perked, Izzy wondered what she could fix for the picnic at the Wilcox township-hall grounds that would be easy and not spoil on a hot day; she decided to open a jar of applesauce and maybe a dish of crabapple pickles and another for dill pickles.

When they finished breakfast, she quickly washed the dishes. Ma came into the kitchen, still in her nightgown. She looked awful. "You all just go without me," she said.

"Aw, ghee, Ma! This is going to be our year to beat Wilcox. I wish you could be there to see it. The excitement would do you good," Izzy told her mother. "Maybe we can take the truck, and you could come later with the car."

"That's right, Ma. You know how to drive now. The kids are pretty good this year," Bud confirmed.

"Go, Cooties, go!" Horace led the little kids in a cheer.

The top of the last inning, and the score was tied; the Cooties were at bat. Jim ran out a ground ball. Harry hit the ball to right field. Mike fouled out to the catcher. The Wilcox pitcher walked the hard-hitting Orville.

Bases loaded and Dell at bat.

"Come on, Dell, hit a homer," cheered the Cooties fans.

Dell stood in, waving the bat.

"Homer, homer, homer," chanted her fans.

"Strike one," the umpire called.

"You were robbed," Izzy yelled from the first base coach's box.

Dell set her feet and glared at the pitcher. "I dare you to pitch that one again." She fouled the next pitch off.

"Strike two," the umpire called.

"Go, Dell, go."

The pitch came in fast and straight. Dell swung and missed.

The Cootie fans all groaned.

"We're doomed," Orville moaned to Izzy. "Janet's up next and she can't hit the broad side of a barn."

"I know," Izzy agreed.

She made a 'T' with her hands and called, "Time out," to the umpire. Orville and Izzy talked it over.

"Let's put Horace in. He's short and might get a walk," Izzy suggested.

"Good idea," Orv agreed, "but then he'd have to play right field."

"Janet's not that good either. I can play a little to the right of center and back him up if the ball comes that way."

"Well, okay, but this better work."

"Horace, you bat for Janet. Now don't even swing at the ball. You're short, so the pitcher will probably walk you," Izzy told him.

"Awe ghee Izzy, I wanted to bat," Janet begged.

"Sorry, Janet, this one's for the team."

Horace stood in. Wilcox fans moaned.

"Time out." Their catcher walked out to talk to the pitcher.

"Time in."

The pitcher moved halfway to home base.

"Hey, Ump, make him get back where he belongs," Izzy called. The pitcher returned to his place.

The first pitch flew high over Horace's head.

"Ball one."

The second pitch rolled on the ground.

"Ball two."

The third pitch almost hit the little guy. When he fell to avoid the pitch, the bat swung over the plate.

"Strike one."

The next pitch came in way wide.

"Ball three."

"I give up," their pitcher hollered to the catcher. "We'll just have to get a couple runs when we bat." Horace walked, and one run scored. Then Jack hit a fly ball. Inning over and Crabapple Creek was up by one.

The bottom of the final inning. Horace took his place in right field.

"Don't worry," Izzy told him. "I'll back you up."

Wilcox had two outs and runners on second and third as their best hitter came up.

"Die, Cooties, die," shouted the Wilcox fans.

"Strike him out, Mike," echoed the Cootie fans.

Their big hitter fouled off the first two pitches.

"Strike two."

"Mike, Mike, Mike."

"Die, Cooties, die."

Mike delivered the pitch.

Crack! The ball rose high in the air toward right field. Izzy and Horace ran for it. Cootie fans groaned.

"I got it! I got it!" Horace shouted. Izzy ran behind him.

The ball hit his outstretched hands and bounced up in the air. Izzy dove and caught it just before it hit the ground.

Cootie fans jeered, "Die, Wilcox!"

Izzy looked up from the cheering teammates and saw Ma on the sideline, clapping and cheering.

# Chapter 31

Monday morning, Miss Webb held up a letter. "Playday was fun. Now it's time to get back to work. Mr. Short, the county superintendent has advised us of the times and places for seventh and eighth grades to take the state-required year-end tests. All eligible seventh and eighth graders in Wilcox Township will report to Wilcox School before 9:00 AM on Saturday, the twentieth of May and Saturday, the twenty-seventh of May."

"Seventh graders must pass all subjects with a grade of 75 percent or better, to be promoted to eighth grade. Eighth graders must pass all subjects to graduate. Arithmetic and agriculture tests will be in the morning and language and reading in the afternoon of the twentieth. Physiology, U.S. history, civics, writing, and spelling tests will be taken on the twenty-seventh."

"I am being tested, too, you know, to see if I have done a good job of teaching. Starting today, we'll review all the important lessons that we should have learned this past eight-and-a-half months. Does anyone have a question?"

"Does that mean that the rest of us are finished for the year?" Irene asked.

The teacher looked stern. "Absolutely not; all the other grades will review and take final tests that I give. You must get 75 percent or better on all subjects, to be promoted."

All week long, everyone shuffled through their books, worked problems, and wrote long lists of spelling words.


Saturday morning, Izzy hopped out of bed, put on her new dress, and ran downstairs to get breakfast. She sneezed a time or two, and her nose drizzled. At least, Ma had been feeling a little better every morning.

Subjects, predicates, verbs, adverbs, multiplication tables, percentage, history dates, the Constitution, and the amendments rattled around in Izzy's head.

At breakfast, Pa added a little extra to the blessing, asking God to smile on Izzy and help her remember the answers to the questions. Bud volunteered to drive her to Wilcox School when Pa said he could take the big family car.

"Thank you, Pa. I want to look my best today," Izzy said.

As she jumped out of the car, she bumped into Janet. "How come you're here?"

"Surprise, surprise," Janet said. While you were being so busy doing sixth grade tests and seventh grade lessons, I was secretly taking seventh grade work. Miss Webb says if I can pass the state tests, I can be in eighth grade with you next year—if you pass." Izzy's mouth dropped open, but she closed it quickly. She knew Janet had noticed her surprise, from the faint, smug smile on her face.

Twenty or thirty students milled around outside. When the bell rang, they went into the building. Wilcox, the biggest school in the township, had seats for thirty students, but one-third of them were too small for the larger seventh and eighth graders. Izzy found herself scrunched at one of the little desks.

At noon, Izzy, and Janet found a place on a cellar windowsill outside, to eat their dinners. Izzy's nose ran. She covered her nose and mouth when she sneezed.


Sunday morning when she woke up, she felt hot and achy. When Pa saw her red face and eyes, he called Dr. Hull. After the call, Pa looked in her mouth and sent her right back to bed. "You have a case of the measles."

"How can you tell?" Izzy asked.

"You have little blue spots inside your mouth. That's a sure sign, the doctor told me."

*Now, where did I get measles?* Izzy wondered. *Maybe it was at Playday, or it could have been at Sunday-School. Last week, one of the girls was sneezing. No one at our school had any problems that I noticed.*

Izzy stayed in bed all day. The light hurt her eyes, so she pulled the shade down. Monday, the county health officer came and nailed a red cardboard sign with big black letters beside the porch door. It said that anyone who had not had the measles could not enter or leave. Bud asked Pa if that meant him. Pa thought maybe Bud had had measles several years ago but couldn't remember, so he said he should stay home.

By Tuesday, when Izzy got up to pee in the slop jar, she saw her face in the mirror. Big red blotches scattered all over her face. She felt awful. Her eyes hurt, and she itched everywhere.

Bud surprised her when he brought her a glass of milk and some cookies. He even volunteered to empty the slop jar. She didn't feel like eating but thanked him anyway.

Each day, the rash grew worse, and it covered her whole body. She slept a lot. Bud brought her cold water to drink and a wet cloth to put on her face and cover her eyes. Ma felt better in the afternoons and washed Izzy's body in warm water mixed with soda. Then, she sprinkled cornstarch on the rash. Izzy felt better for an hour or two, until it started itching again. She forgot all about school and tests and everything. She wished she could die.

By Saturday, she felt a little better, but by then, Bud had come down with the measles too. Izzy suddenly realized that she should be taking tests at Wilcox School. *I wonder if Janet is there. Janet will be in eighth grade next year if she passes all the tests. Missing the last five tests means I will have to do seventh grade all over again.*

That night, she felt a lot better and went downstairs for supper. While they waited for Pa to finish milking, she confided her problem to Ma. The more Izzy thought about it, the more she wanted to do something. Monday she got up enough courage to look up the phone number of the county superintendent. "Ma, can I please call Mr. Short in Riverton? Maybe he can tell me what to do."

"Well, you know it costs a dime to make a long distance call, but okay, if you think it will help," Ma said reluctantly.

A secretary answered the phone, and Izzy explained the problem. The secretary said she would have Mr. Short call back. Izzy waited all day, but no phone call. She didn't dare ask Ma if she could make another ten-cent call. The wait upset her. Finally, at ten the next morning, the phone rang.

"I checked the master list," the superintendent told her. "I called your teacher, Miss Webb. She told me that you were an excellent student and asked me to help you. The ladies marking the test will be finished Wednesday, so the grades can be mailed out in time for the county graduation ceremony. If you can come into my office before then, we'll give you the tests here in my office."

"Thank you, Mr. Short. I'll be there." She hung up.

"Wednesday—today is Tuesday. That doesn't leave much time."

At supper, she explained the problem to Pa. He agreed to take her to the county seat the next morning and pick her up later. "It's been so dry this spring, with no rain since March. There's no sense even trying to cultivate corn. Not even the weeds are growing," he said.

# Chapter 32

About 2 AM on Wednesday morning, Izzy woke up to the sound of a cow bellowing in the barn. She knew that sound. It meant that a cow was delivering a calf. By 6 AM, the bellowing grew loader and more frequent. Izzy hurried to dress and ran downstairs. Pa was on the phone calling the veterinarian.

"I think the calf is stuck in the birth canal. Maybe you can turn it for me," he said.

Izzy's heart sank. Pa wouldn't be able to drive her to Riverton. Bud couldn't drive her because he had the measles. That left Ma. Ma had never driven in the city and might not feel that she could.

Ma came into the kitchen in her nightgown. "I haven't had a wink of sleep since two o'clock. That poor cow—why does God have to make all females suffer so to have babies, just because Eve ate that old apple? It just isn't fair."

"Oh, Ma, you don't really believe that old story about Eve coming from Adam's rib and stuff? A rib doesn't look anything like a woman," Izzy said.

"Well, it's in the Bible. It makes as much sense as thinking we all came from monkeys."

Izzy didn't want to argue. She decided to tell Ma her own problem.

Ma was sympathetic. She said she felt better but didn't feel well enough to try to drive in the city and didn't know where she could go or what she would do all day.

"Can you at least take me as far as the end of the streetcar tracks? You can come right home, and I'll take the streetcar the rest of the way," Izzy begged, as she lit the kerosene stove to make oatmeal.

"Well, I guess I could do that, but how would you get home?"

"Maybe the cow will be delivered by then, and Pa can come get me."

"Just don't make any coffee or fry any bacon. Maybe Bud would like some oatmeal, and I think maybe I can eat some too," Ma said.


Ma stopped the car at the edge of the city when she saw the overhead wires and iron rails of the streetcar. She fished in her purse and gave Izzy two dimes. "One is for the streetcar, and the other is for the phone call when you are finished. Now, are you sure you'll be okay?"

"Don't worry Ma; I'll be just fine. Look, here comes a streetcar now."

Izzy watched as the motorman pulled the trolley pole down on one end of the car and put up another one at the other end. She jumped in the open door. The conductor was moving the backs of the seat to face the opposite direction. He took her dime, and she told him this was her first ride on a streetcar.

"Don't worry, Miss. Where are you going?"

"To the County Superintendent of Schools."

"That's right on this route. It's in the courthouse. I'll let you know when to get off."

Izzy studied the big signboard at the entrance to the courthouse. The numbers and names of ten or fifteen offices were listed on the sign. She found "310 Superintendent of Schools."

She walked down the long hall, looking at the numbers on the doors. The last number said 110. She looked around to see if there was another hall. Walking back, she looked in an open door that said "103 River County Court." Ten or twelve ladies sat around two big tables with stacks of papers in front of them.

In the middle of the hall, across from the front door, she saw a big open stairway. She climbed all the way to the third floor before she found room 310.

She knocked lightly and heard someone say, "Come in."

"Yes, what can I do for you?" asked an older lady with gray hair pulled back in a tight bun.

"Mr. Short told me on the phone that I could take the last five seventh grade tests," Izzy said, as she cautiously entered the cluttered room.

"Oh yes. He asked me to watch for you. Just come on in and have a seat at this little table in the corner." The lady handed her a large envelope. "When you are finished with the first test, let me know, and I'll give you the second one. Don't waste any time. It's already after nine. I have to get them downstairs to the courtroom for the ladies to correct before they finish at five."

Izzy opened the first test and started. She hurried and made too many mistakes. *I'd better slow down and get it right the first time, or I'll never get finished,* she thought. She didn't even take time to eat the sandwich she had brought in a paper sack. By four-thirty she was ready for the last test, which was spelling. Mr. Short was at his desk, and he read the spelling words for her—one hundred words. Spelling was Izzy's least favorite subject.

By a quarter to five she was finished. She wanted to go over the answers but was afraid to ask because time was running out, so she just silently said a little prayer and offered Mr. Short her second dime to call Pa.

# Chapter 33

Izzy saw a cloud of dust coming from the west and ran to the mailbox. Every day for the past week, she had done the same thing. *Please, let it come today,* she prayed. When the mailman handed her the envelope, she tore it open.

Agriculture 82

Arithmetic 86

Civics 90

Language 79

Physiology 87

Reading 81

Spelling 75

U.S. History 91

Writing 78

"Ma, Ma, I passed," she hollered, as she ran through the kitchen door.

"That's wonderful." Ma smiled. "I know it means so much to you. Now, I hope you can get your mind onto all the work around here. I'm going to need all the help I can get."

"Why do you say that?"

"I think I'm going to have a baby."

Before Izzy could say anything, Janet banged on the kitchen door and came in without waiting to be asked. "Izzy, I passed! I passed! Did you pass?" Izzy nodded. "Wonderful. Now we can be friends again." Janet hugged Izzy. Izzy was puzzled by Janet's remark. She thought they had always been friends. *Well, I had been a little jealous because Janet had so many pretty dresses and prettier hair. Maybe she was jealous because I skipped sixth grade.*

"Come see what Grandpa and Grandma brought me from Chicago." Janet grabbed Izzy by the hand. A bright blue bicycle leaned against the porch steps. "Somebody bought it and couldn't make the payments, so Grandpa's bank had to take it back. I'm so happy; I'm not even going to be mad at you for giving me the measles. They weren't bad at all, and now I don't have to worry about ever getting them again. I heard you had to take your tests in Riverton. I got to hurry and get home. I want to call everybody I know, but I just had to tell you in person and show you my bike." Finally, she stopped talking to get her breath.

Izzy didn't even know that Janet had had measles. *Was that what she meant about being friends again?* Before she could get a word in edgewise, Janet was gone. *I'm glad she's gone. I want to ask Ma about what she just said.* When she re-entered the kitchen, Ma was on the telephone.

Izzy decided it was going to be a long conversation. *It must be that gabby old Mrs. O'Malley.* Ma just kept repeating, "Uh-huh," and "really."

Izzy got her basket and headed for her rounds, to collect the eggs and do her evening chores. She stopped at the barn to watch the kittens when Bud squirted them in the mouth with milk straight from the cows, then went to the well for a pail of fresh water for supper. She had to hurry to fill the tank in the kerosene stove, so they could make supper.

By the time she finished, Bud and Pa had come into the kitchen. Ma's one sentence had burned a hole in her brain. *A baby? Ma is too old to have a baby. My life will never be the same. I'll probably be stuck with some squalling brat of a brother. Ma will expect me to take care of the baby or else do all the cooking and cleaning and washing and everything else. How could this happen? Now, we'll never have enough money for me to go to the university and be an engineer.*

That night, she didn't have a chance to see Ma alone to ask more about the baby.

As soon as she heard the milking machine start the next morning, Izzy snuck into Ma's and Pa's bedroom. Ma was awake, so she crawled into bed with her. It had been years since she had done that.

"Did you say you're having a baby?" she asked.

"I'm not sure, but I think so. At first, I just thought it was the start of the change of life, but when I started being sick in the morning, I was really scared," Ma said. "I'm going to see Dr. Hull tomorrow and make sure, but I think he's going to agree. I know you'll be a good sister."

"I'm scared too. I don't know anything about babies. Do Pa and Bud know this?"

"Pa does, but not Bud. Just be sure you don't tell anyone until we know for sure. Do you promise?"

"I promise."


"Izzy, can you come over to my house?" Janet asked her on the phone. "I have something to show you." Izzy had just finished the dinner dishes, and Ma was taking a nap. She wrote Ma a note, grabbed the bridle from the barn, and whistled for Prince at the pasture gate.

Janet led Izzy upstairs to her room. "Ingrid got a job working for Dr. Hull."

"Is she a nurse now?" Izzy asked.

"Oh no, nothing like that; she just answers the phone and greets the patients. Sometimes she washes the instruments, and she sweeps the floor and dusts the furniture. But the best part is that she can read any of the doctor's books. She snuck one home for me. Come see."

Izzy and Janet flopped, bellies down, on the big double bed that Janet shared with her sister, Ingrid. Janet reached under her pillow and took out a book called 'Obstetrics for Nurses'. She opened it to the page that showed four different pictures. The first picture showed a baby being born. The top of a baby's head with wet hair made Izzy's eyes open wide. It said "normal birth position." Another picture showed a foot coming out. Still another picture showed the baby's rear end and another showed the baby's face. "Ugh!" *No wonder Ma's scared.*

They shuffled through more pages, oohing and aahing at each new picture. When they heard Mrs. Andrews coming up the steps, Janet shoved the book back under the pillow and changed the subject. "My bosoms are now big enough to fill one of Ingrid's starter bras."

Mrs. Andrews came in with a plate of cookies and two glasses of milk. Izzy loved Mrs. Andrews' delicious Swedish spritz cookies, and she thanked her. The girls sat on the wide windowsill, eating cookies. They continued the conversation where they left off before Janet's mother came in.

"Big deal," Izzy said. "Who wants tits anyway? Mine hurt, and Bud teases me all the time about them."

"Oh, Izzy, that's because he's a guy. He's turning into a man. Guys love girls with big bosoms. You should be happy."

"Let's change the subject. Bud says he thinks someone is moving into the old Simpson house that's way back in the field behind the O'Malley's. You know, it's kind of run-down. Nobody has lived there for years. He said he saw the gate to the lane that runs back there open and the grass all beat down like cars or something had been through."

"I wonder if there are any kids. We need some new faces around here. Let's go see." Janet jumped up and motioned for Izzy to follow.

Izzy mounted Prince, and Janet pedaled her new bike. They rode down the lane overgrown with weeds. Bushes grew on both sides, so they couldn't see the house until suddenly, there it was.

A girl, who looked about their age, with short black hair sat on the back step with a big, black, mean-looking dog. She didn't look too happy.

An old truck with a closed box stood by the door. The sign on the side said GAMBOLI BROTHERS—FRESH FRUIT and VEGETABLES, Chicago, Illinois.

A black coupe stood under a tree, with its hood folded back. A pair of legs below a boy's butt showed someone tinkering with the engine. Izzy dismounted and walked over to the car.

"Is that a new Ford V-8?" she asked.

"Sure is." A boy about her age pulled his head out, turned around, and looked her over. "Well, hello. I'm Alexander

Gamboli—Alex for short. Who are you?" He had black curly hair, dark eyes, and a smile that made Izzy's legs weak.

"I'm Isabelle Norton—Izzy for short." *But why do boys always seem to look at my chest and not my face?*

With introductions over, Izzy looked at the motor. "I've never seen so many spark plugs on one car. Is she real fast?"

"You bet. My Uncle Giuseppe is a top mechanic. He's teaching me everything he knows about cars."

"I wish I had an Uncle Giuseppe. I want to know everything about cars, but nobody wants to teach me."

Alex looked at Izzy and smiled. "Hey, I'd be glad to teach you. Most girls don't care anything about cars."

While Izzy talked to Alex, Janet walked over toward the girl. The black dog barked at her.

"Shut up, Killer," the girl commanded. The dog quit barking but glared; a low growl scared poor Janet, who couldn't take another step.

"I'm Janet Andrews, one of your neighbors. We came over to say hello," she said, nodding toward Izzy.

"Well, I'm Gina. I can't say I'm thrilled to be living in this godforsaken, hick-infested place." The girl frowned. Janet didn't know what to say. She just stood there with her mouth open.

A man came out of the back door and called to Alex. "Come here," he hollered.

"Got to go," Alex said. "Glad to meet you. Come again sometime."

Izzy felt sure the man didn't want them there. She hollered to Janet, "Let's go, Jan. Bye, Alex."

Janet backed away but kept her eyes on the dog until she joined Izzy.

"What a grouch! She's sour as a green crabapple," Janet said, as they retreated down the lane.

# Chapter 34

Izzy noticed that the sun was getting lower in the west. *I better get home and help Ma get supper.* At the corner, Janet kept going, and Izzy turned east. As she came close to home, a cloud of dust approached her. She turned her head to see who it was, as she guided Prince to the side to let the car go by. She made out that it was a Duisenberg. It had chrome all over. Chrome pipes even came out the side of the long hood. "Wow."

When she reached home, she pulled the bridle off Prince, threw it over the gatepost of the pasture, and opened the gate. "Go get a drink from the creek," she told him with a slap on his butt. Just then, she saw the Duisenberg turn into the driveway, but she didn't take time to check it out. She was late, and Ma would be cranky.

"Dear Father in heaven, bless this food we are about to eat," Pa prayed, as they sat at the supper table. "And dear Lord, please send us some rain, so that we will have food for our animals this winter. Amen."

"What did the guy in the Duisenberg want?" Izzy asked, as the food was being passed around.

"He wanted to buy Prince. I told him the pony belonged to my daughter and was not for sale."

"Oh, I couldn't sell Prince," Izzy gasped. "He's worth more than all the money in the world."

"Well, it is your decision," Pa said." I gave him our phone number and told him to call back in the morning."

The rest of the family chattered on, as Izzy thought about her pony. Before the meal ended, Izzy asked, "How much did he say he would pay?"

"He offered fifty dollars."

"Fifty dollars—that's a lot of money."

Everyone fell quiet as they ate. Pa finally spoke. "I think I may have to sell most of the cows. It looks like there isn't going to be any harvest this year because of the drought. There's enough hay left in the barn to carry over the team and a few milk cows."

Izzy looked up. "Will the man in the Duisenberg be sure that Prince gets enough to eat?"

"He's a very rich man from Chicago, I think. He said he has one of those big mansions over on Lake Geneva. His crippled son saw you riding today and begged him to buy the pony. The boy is recovering from infantile paralysis. The poor kid is really down. The guy assured me he has a caretaker and can buy plenty of hay and oats, so Prince would get very good care."

Izzy broke another long silence. "Fifty dollars would go a long way toward the cost of the new baby."

"Baby!"

Milk spewed out of Bud's nose and mouth, making a mess on his plate, the table, and the floor.

"Izzy, I didn't think you had it in you."

Ma gasped, "Bud, you don't mean that. How could you think that of Izzy?"

"Oh, it's not me; it's Ma," Izzy said at the same time.

"Isabelle, you promised." Ma gaped at Izzy.

"Sorry, Ma, it just slipped out," Izzy apologized.

"Well, alright. He would know sooner or later anyway, I guess," Ma said.


Poor Izzy's brain buzzed inside her head.

Drought, sell the cows, a new baby, Alex, no hay, no oats, crippled rich boy, Prince, no hay, new baby—these thoughts all rattled around in her head, bumping into each other, as she wiped the dishpan and hung it on the nail at the end of the cabinet.

# Chapter 35

In the sitting room, Pa read the paper beside the bright gasoline lamp, and Ma sat in her rocking chair, darning Bud's socks. Bud was off somewhere, probably chasing some girl. Izzy wandered outside and looked at the full moon peeking over the horizon.

Walking to the pasture gate, she whistled for Prince. She let him out and closed the gate. The bridle still hung on the gatepost, and she put it on the pony. They headed up the road. When they came to the edge of the woods, the rising moon cast a shadow over the road. A hundred feet farther east, a bright spot broke the shadow showing where the bridge crossed over Crabapple Creek.

Izzy got a spooky feeling, remembering Icabod and Brom Bones. Thinking about the Halloween play made her laugh. At the bridge, she looked up the creek. The creek should have been ten feet wide there, but because of the dry summer, only a narrow stream of water trickled in the middle. In the moonlight, the creek bed showed on either side of the stream, with only a few rocks lying around. *Ghee, that looks like a great pathway through the thick woods.* "Let's go exploring, Prince," she told the pony. Prince jumped the ditch, and they headed up the sandy creek bottom. *I've never been up Crabapple Creek this far before. I wonder where the water comes from.*

Just as they came out of the woods at the top of the hill, Izzy heard men's voices and heard motors running. Not sure where she was, she turned back into the woods. In the moonlight, she made out the old Simpson place. Men were taking boxes out of the vegetable truck and loading them into several cars.

A dog started barking. Izzy knew it was the same dog they had seen that afternoon. "What is it, Killer?" the man asked.

*We better get out of here in a hurry,* she thought, and pulled Prince's head around by the reins. Just then, one of the pony's shoes broke a stick with a loud crack. As they hurried back down the creek bed, she heard what sounded like a shotgun.

With Prince safely back in his own pasture, Izzy got into bed without taking off her overalls. She didn't tell Pa or Ma about being shot at, because she knew she shouldn't have been out riding Prince at night.

Curled up in a ball, the events of the day raced around in her brain. By morning, she awoke with a start. *I must have been dreaming. Why do they move fruit and vegetables at night? Why don't they deliver them in the truck in the daytime? Why did that man shoot at the sound of a stick breaking? It could have been a deer or some other night animal.*

# Chapter 36

At breakfast, she hardly touched her food. "It will be okay to sell Prince," Izzy announced. "I'm getting too old for a pony anyway. I would rather have a bike like Janet." She looked at Pa. "With hay and oats running out, he'll be better fed by that rich man."

After finishing the breakfast dishes, she hurried to the pasture gate, stopping at the withering garden to pull a puny carrot and wiped it on her overall leg. "Sorry, Prince old boy, It's the best I could do," she said, holding out the sorry treat when he came to her whistle. The man with the Duisenberg had called and said he would be at their place in an hour to get the pony.

Izzy took the currycomb and the brush and groomed Prince until his coat shone. "You're a good looking pony. I want that poor little rich kid to appreciate you. Maybe you can help the boy get better."

When the new model Hudson truck entered the yard, it was covered with dust. While the rich man gave Pa two twenty-dollar bills and a ten, Izzy slipped the bridle on Prince. A small boy slid out of the truck on his crutches and hobbled over to where Prince watched him. *I wonder what the pony is thinking. I told him he was going to have a new owner, but I don't know if he understood,* Izzy mused.

The truck driver lifted the boy onto the pony's bare back, and she handed him the reins. The pony looked at the boy. Izzy stroked Prince's fuzzy nose and whispered, "Its okay. He's your new owner now."

She started to lead the little horse. The boy lost his balance and would have fallen, except the man caught him. "It's all right, Percy. We'll get you a nice saddle, and your mama will teach you how to ride."

With Prince safely in the back of the truck, Percy insisted on riding beside his new friend. The rich man got in the back of the truck with his son, and they drove off, leaving only a cloud of dust.

Izzy couldn't look. She swallowed hard on the lump in her throat but couldn't quite make it go away. She started running as fast as she could. When she got to the woods, she dropped to the ground and cried.

# Chapter 37

"The truck will be here to take the cows to the stock market in Chicago this morning," Pa announced a few days later at breakfast.

Ma and Izzy watched from the porch as each cow was led up the shaky wooden ramp into the waiting cattle truck. Some went without any trouble. Others refused. Sweat poured off Pa's dusty face, leaving tracks in his three days growth of whiskers. Sweat wet his shirt. Bud helped by pushing the cows from behind. Some of the stubborn cows kicked out with a hind leg. One hoof hit Bud right in the stomach, and another stepped on his foot. Both Bud and Pa used bad words. Ma frowned every time she heard them, and Izzy tried to remember them. *Maybe they'll come in handy later. I'll have to ask Bud what they mean when Ma can't hear.*

It took almost an hour to load the cows. When the truck drove away, Pa turned his back to the house and walked to the well for a drink of water. Izzy went into the house. She didn't want to see Pa just then.

Izzy thought about where the cows were going and wondered how long it would be before they showed up at The Mercantile as bologna. *Oh well, I don't like bologna anyway, and we can't afford it.*

"All right, all right, let's get to work," Pa barked at Bud and Izzy. "Just because there's no harvest this year doesn't mean we can lie around and do nothing. There's a lot of junk around the place that needs to be picked up and hauled away, so let's get busy."

Bud and Izzy started loading old cans and odd pieces of junk into Bud's old model 'T' truck. They even went into the loft of the shed. "There's too much junk up here for this load. We'll get it some other day," Bud said.

"Just a minute." Izzy saw lots of interesting stuff. "Maybe there is something here we can use for the baby."

"Oh come on. Everything is too dirty and probably falling apart." Bud went down the ladder followed by Izzy. *I'll come back later*, she told herself.

"Come on and ride to the dump with me," Bud called.

"I might as well. Maybe someone has thrown away some neat junk that I can practice fixing."

They threw their stuff over the edge of the deep gravel pit that had run out of gravel. It was half-full of all kinds of old junk from all over the Wilcox Township. Izzy looked down and saw a bicycle about to be covered with the things they tossed in. She jumped into the pit and slid on the seat of her overalls down the steep slope. She climbed over busted wagon wheels, tin cans, old tires, and a hundred other pieces of junk until she reached the broken bike.

Looking it over, she groaned. It had flat tires and a bent frame. The chain was broken, and one pedal was missing. Bud stood at the top of the pit, laughing at her.

"Cut it out, and help me," she hollered.

Still laughing, he got back in the truck, brought out a rope, and threw one end down to her. She tied it to the bent frame. Bud pulled the bike up, while Izzy crawled on hands and knees to the edge of the pit, where Bud helped her over the edge.

"Oh boy, you're a better mechanic than I think you are if you can make that thing work," her brother said.


On the way home, she told Bud about what she had seen at the Simpson place the other night. "Why would anyone be loading fruit and vegetables at night?"

"Maybe it isn't cabbage and potatoes, you know," he responded.

"What else could they be hauling that they would do it at night?"

"Probably something illegal."

"What do you mean?" she asked.

"Haven't you ever heard of the 18th amendment?"

"I've heard about it but don't exactly know what it's all about."

"The 18th amendment made it illegal to make or sell alcoholic beverages, but it's unfair. If the people want something, why should the government say they can't have it? Maybe if Mr. Roosevelt gets elected president, he'll get that old amendment repealed."

"I'm not quite sure what alcoholic beverages are. Pa put some stinky stuff he called wood alcohol in the car radiator last winter, so it wouldn't freeze. He said if anyone drank it, they would go blind. Why would anyone want to drink something that would make them blind?"

"Wood alcohol is poison," Bud said. "The law is about beer and whiskey and wine and rum and stuff. That's what people like to drink."

"Why?"

"'Cause it tastes good and makes them happy, I guess."

"What's wrong with that?" Izzy felt confused.

"You sure are dumb. You don't know much about what goes on in the world, do you?"

"Well, I'm always washing the supper dishes in the kitchen while the rest of the family listens to the news on the radio in the sitting room."

"Ma is always preaching to me about the evils of alcohol. She calls it booze." Bud knew all the answers. "She says it makes people do crazy stuff and fall down and puke. She claims they get so they will buy it when they should use their money to buy food for their families. That's ridiculous. I hope they'll repeal that old law some day. I'm going to try beer and whiskey when I get a chance to see if it's as good as my buddies say it is, even if Ma doesn't approve."

"But what has that to do with the Gambolis? Why would they be hauling and unloading something in a run-down place like the old Simpson house in the middle of the night?"

"Have you ever heard about Chicago gangsters? They form gangs. Sometimes gangs kill each other because they make big money hauling and selling illegal liquor. They will kill to keep a rival gang from butting into their territory. They hide from the law and from other gangs. That's why they keep moving around and hole up in hidden places."

"Do you think the Gambolis are gangsters?

"Maybe, they're from Chicago aren't they? Bootleggers bring booze from other countries like Canada. Take some advice from your big brother, little girl; don't have anything to do with those Gambolis."

# Chapter 38

Bicycle parts lay all around Izzy. She sat in the shade of the burr oak tree beside the shed on an upturned nail keg and stared at them.

Ma and Pa had gone to town to see the doctor, and Izzy had spent two hours taking the old bike apart and laying each piece on a newspaper in the exact order that she had removed it.

*What do I do now? Everything looks worn-out or broken.* Just then, she heard a boy's voice.

Hello. Alex took two bananas from the basket of his bicycle as he leaned it on the tree." I brought us something to eat," he said, offering her one of the bananas.

Izzy took it and mumbled, "Thank you." In her mind, she was thinking, *His family really are fruit dealers. That sounds much better than gangsters.* She had seen bananas hanging from the ceiling of The Mercantile but had never eaten one. Ma always said they couldn't afford such luxuries.

She looked at both ends but didn't know how to open the fruit. She decided to wait and see what Alex did and follow his lead. Before he had a chance, though, Janet rode up on her bicycle.

"Well, hello, Goldilocks," Alex joked. "Have you busted up any bear family furniture today?"

"Of course not," Janet replied. "That's such a dumb story. Proper girls don't go around walking into other people's houses unless they're invited."

Alex hadn't opened his banana yet, so he offered it to Janet. She broke off one end and pulled back the peeling. Izzy did the same thing to hers.

"Izzy, I've studied the Constitution of the United States. Using it for a guide, I've written a preamble for our Friday Afternoon Society's new constitution. Do you want to hear it?" Not waiting for an answer, she pulled a piece of paper from her pocket and started reading.

"We, the students of Crabapple Creek Elementary School, in order to form a more perfect organization, establish fairness for all students, insure good conduct, and provide for the common good of all, do ordain and establish this constitution for 'The Crabapple Creek Friday Afternoon Society'."

Alex looked puzzled. "What's that all about?" he asked Izzy.

"Janet is on the committee to write some rules for the club we have at school," Izzy told him. "I'm the president. That's great, Janet. At the first meeting in September, we'll run it by the rest of the kids and see what they think. Right now, I'm trying to fix up this old bike I found, so I can ride around like you and Alex. You know that I sold the Prince, don't you?" Izzy said.

"Well, if you're more interested in that old wreck," Janet said, pointing to the bicycle parts, "than our new constitution, I guess I'll just go home and leave you two alone to play with a pile of junk." She rode off in a huff.

"She's a spunky little thing, isn't she?" Alex remarked with a big smile. "Now about this bike—let's see what we can do."

He picked up the frame. "It looks like it's been run over by a truck. Maybe we can straighten it, though." He laid it down and picked up the chain. "But you'll have to buy a new chain. This one is missing half its links." Every part he picked up had something wrong with it. At last, he shook his head. "It would cost more to fix up this old wreck than to buy a new one."

Izzy shook her head. She knew he was right, but she didn't want to admit it. She suggested they get a drink of cold water from the well. She passed the community dipper to

Alex while she pumped the handle. As he took a deep drink of fresh, cool water, Pa and Ma drove into the driveway.

"Well, I got to go Izzy. I'll see you later. Maybe I can find some old part around our place." He handed her the dipper and rode away, leaving a trail of dust.

Pa drove the car right up to the steps by the back porch. He ran around the car and helped Ma out. *That's funny. He's never done that before.* Izzy had a funny feeling in her stomach.

# Chapter 39

Izzy ran to the house from the well. When she entered the kitchen, she heard talking in the bedroom. She knew something must be wrong. She put her ear to the closed door to hear what Ma and Pa were saying.

Ma seemed to be crying. Pa sounded funny. He sounded sort of consoling, like he did when she'd hurt her knee or something. Then, everything turned quiet. The door opened, and Izzy fell into Pa.

"Learn anything?" he asked, setting her straight.

"Is something wrong, Pa?" Izzy asked.

"I'm not sure." he replied. "The doctor says your ma's blood pressure is too high, and the pee sample has something called albumin. He says it isn't good. He thinks she may be getting what he called 'clamp' something or other. She'll have to stay in bed, drink lots of water, and cut out salt. She shouldn't get excited until the baby is born." He sighed and turned to Izzy. "You can go bring some fresh well water for her right now."

Izzy got the water and filled a pitcher. She took it with a glass into the bedroom and set them on the table beside the bed. Ma opened her eyes. They looked red from crying, but she managed a weak smile. "Thank you."

Izzy made supper that night without waiting for Ma to tell her what to fix. Pa's blessing was longer than usual. He covered the dry season and the pony; and spent at least two whole minutes on Ma, asking the Lord to help their family. Bud and Izzy didn't mind the long prayer. They silently prayed along with Pa.

As they passed the food, Bud and Izzy asked a thousand questions. Bud volunteered to do the outside work. "Since we only have three cows, I can milk them by hand and save money running the milking machine. You and Izzy can take care of Ma and the house," he said to Pa.

"Izzy, you're almost thirteen. Maybe you can be the nurse and take care of your Ma. Then I can do the cooking and take care of the house," Pa said.

"But I don't know the first thing about nursing or babies and stuff like that," Izzy said.

Pa frowned. "It wouldn't be proper for me to be the nurse, you know."

*Why not?* Izzy thought but didn't say anything. *He takes care of sick cows.*

"Could we at least take turns caring for Ma and doing the cooking and the dishes?" Izzy asked.

"I think it would be better for you to take care of changing the bed every day and helping her bathe. As hot as it is, she'll sweat a lot and need a bath and clean sheets every day. I'll do the laundry. Then, we can take turns in the afternoon, sitting with her in case she needs anything, and the other one will get supper."

Izzy felt confused and scared but agreed to try. In the morning, she took a pan of warm water with a washrag, soap, and a towel into the bedroom. Somehow, she managed to make Ma comfortable. Ma even talked more than usual.

That afternoon, while Izzy sat with Ma, she looked out the window and saw Alex coming down the road on his bike. Ma was asleep, so she tiptoed to the kitchen door as not to wake her.

"I brought you a pear," Alex said, handing her the fruit.

"Oh thank you," Izzy answered, speaking very low. "Do you mind if I save it for Ma? The doctor says she has to stay in bed until after the baby is born, and she can't have anything with salt in it."

"Oh sure, here, she can have mine too," he whispered.

"I'm going to throw that old bike in the junk barrel," Izzy told him. "Pa and I are taking turns sitting with Ma in the afternoon, and I need to get back to her. Come see me tomorrow if you want to."

"Sounds good, I'll see you." He rode off.

The next afternoon, Alex drove into the driveway with the V-8 coupe and a large lady with a red face and gray hair pulled back in a bun. When Izzy came to the kitchen door, he introduced her to his mama.

"When I told Mama about your mother needing to stay in bed and about the baby and all, she insisted I bring her over with some good Italian food. There's salt in it, but the rest of the family can eat it. That should spare them from having to eat your cooking." They both laughed.

Izzy called Pa, who came out and thanked them as he took the big pan of spaghetti. "Mrs. Norton is awake and would like to meet you," he said.

While Alex's mama visited with Ma, Izzy and Alex sat on the porch steps and talked. Izzy told him about wanting to go to the university and be an engineer, and he told her about how he loved machinery and some day wanted to learn to fly an airplane.

When the company left, Pa told Ma about the food. Her first reaction was to say no. "We can't accept charity."

"It's not charity," he said. "They're just being good neighbors. We don't want to hurt their feelings. We can give them some fresh milk and eggs in exchange. They don't have any chickens or cows, and there isn't enough milk to sell from our three cows anyway."

Bud was surprised at supper by the great spaghetti. "Did you cook this, Pa?" he asked.

Izzy wondered if Pa thought the Gambolis were gangsters.

Ma liked Mama Gamboli from the first time they met. Alex brought Mama G. every afternoon to visit. That gave Izzy time to talk to Alex, and she looked forward to their visits.

Before long, the two families fell into a routine. Every afternoon, Alex brought his mama with enough food for the whole family, including some without salt for Ma. Pa gave him a gallon of milk and a dozen eggs. Pa and Izzy liked not having to cook. Everything went well.

One day, while Ma and Mama Gamboli talked to each other, Alex and Izzy poked around in the shed. Alex asked what was in the loft. They climbed the ladder nailed to the outside wall and crawled through the large doorway. The door hung by the top hinge at a crazy angle.

"I'm really concerned about our new baby," Izzy confided in Alex. "Every time I try to talk to Pa about getting stuff together, he just says Ma's too old to have a baby, and because of her illness, the baby won't live anyway. We don't even have a bed to put a baby in or a single diaper."

"Let's look over some of this junk. I bet we might find an old crib left over from when you were a baby." Alex laughed and they started looking over the piles and piles of stuff that had accumulated for years.

Izzy crawled under the low eaves. In the dim light from the door and the holes in the roof of the shed her eyes were able to make out different things. "Hey, look here. I found a box the right size for a baby, but it's full of old gunnysacks. It has faded blue paint on it and what look like red and yellow flowers. I'll bet this might be my cradle."

Together, they dug it out. Sure enough, on the bottom, someone had nailed two rockers from an old rocking chair. "It's kind of dirty, and the rockers could use a few more nails." They threw out the sacks, brushed off most of the dirt and pigeon droppings, and tugged the cradle to the open door. "Alex, you climb down the ladder, and I'll lower it to you. We can clean it up at the tank."

One afternoon, before Alex and his mama arrived, Mrs. O'Malley came to visit.

"Sure and it's a wonderful thing, bringing a new baby into the world. Now, me and my Pat, we've done it thirteen times. Course, three of them are in heaven with the Good Lord." *Bridget O'Malley sure likes to talk.*

"Now, my Lois, she's the baby. Now, she's the last one. I'm all done with that change of life falderal. I was telling my

Pat, I says, 'Pat, we ain't got no use for baby stuff no more. I think I'll just pack it all up and take it over to the Norton's." She opened a paper bag and showed Ma the undershirts, diapers, and the tiny blankets.

"Well, I certainly thank you. I've given all the things I had for Izzy to the Gruders long ago. The Lord knows these will come in handy." Ma held her arms out, and Mrs. O'Malley leaned over the bed for a neighborly hug. "It'll be nice to have the new baby to keep me company. Maybe it will be a girl, and she can help me around the house."

"Before long, I suppose Bud will be getting married, and Izzy wants to go to the university. I don't know how we can manage that with the drought and all." She sighed and looked out the window to hide a tear. "They grow up so fast. But Izzy's so headstrong; she'll find a way." Izzy blushed and pretended she hadn't heard her.

"Faith and be gory, ain't it the truth. My Lois, now she's gonna be goin' to school already. First grade, she even has her own cow to milk each morning. With half the herd sold off, it's not like she's needed in the barn, but she wants to be with Mike and the rest."


Another day, Mrs. Gruder and Dell came to see Ma. Izzy was glad to see them. She hadn't seen Dell since school let out. Visitors always made the day seem a little shorter.

"What ya been doing all summer and how are Jack and the rest of your gang?" Izzy greeted her old friend.

"Well, there ain't no crops or nothing so me and Jack decided to pick up all them stones in the fields. We decided we're gonna build us a new house of stones. We gotta a big pile of them already. You should see the picture Jack drew of the new house. We pasted it right on the kitchen wall so we could all see it while we eat. Even the little kids are helpin."

"With all my young'uns, they've worn out every piece of baby stuff we ever had. We used them for rags mostly," Mrs. Gruder told Ma. "But you and the mister have always been so good to my family. I wanted to bring something for the new baby. I just gathered up a lot of scraps and made a small quilt. I stuffed it with the sides from a worn out blanket."

Ma took the quilt and spread it on the bed in front of her. "It will be perfect," she said. Izzy knew how much Ma hated charity, but down deep knew she was glad to see the neighbors helping.

Izzy got good at giving Ma a bath in bed and enjoyed helping to make her feel better. She enjoyed talking with Ma when they were alone. Ma had quit going on about being so poor all the time. She even seemed to like lying in bed, and she slept a lot.

# Chapter 40

"School starts next Monday. Do you think I should stay home?" Izzy asked Pa at supper. "Ma needs me."

"No, absolutely not," Pa told her. "You and Bud are both going to go to school. Besides, it's the law. If you take care of her personal needs before you go in the morning, I'll pack your dinner pail and take care of her during the day."

Izzy felt torn. She wanted to go to school, but she wanted to take care of Ma too.

The first morning everything went wrong. The water for Ma's bath was too cold. When she heated it, it was too hot. Then, she dropped the soap and had to get under the bed to get it. Ma wanted to talk until Izzy finally had to ask if they could finish the conversation when she got home.

Izzy had just reached the lilac bushes near the school when she heard the bell.

"Ghee, I'm going to be late." *I hate being late on the first day. What if we have a new teacher? She'll think I'm a goof-off.*

She entered the classroom as the kids finished singing 'America'. Miss Webb scowled when Izzy tiptoed in. "There's only one seat left, Isabelle. It's the last one in the left row."

"I'm sorry I'm late," Izzy said. "I had to help Ma. She's not allowed out of bed until our baby comes."

"I understand, so I'll excuse you this time. Maybe you can get your work a little better organized after this," the teacher replied.

"I see we have some new students this year." Miss Webb looked at Susan. "Will you please stand and introduce your brother, Susan?"

Susan stood up and went to the seat where a small, freckled-face boy with sandy hair sat. "This is my little brother, Dan," she said. He likes to eat and play ball."

Mike walked to the seat in front of Dan and said, "My little sister is Lois. She's real smart. She can even milk a cow, and she's only six." Some of the kids clapped.

"Will the young lady in the front of the third row stand up and tell us who you are and a bit about yourself?" The teacher looked at Gina, who stood but didn't turn around.

"My name is Regina Gamboli, and I come from Chicago. For you hicks here in Wisconsin," she turned and looked at the room full of students, "that's the second biggest city in the country. We have everything there, including electricity, bathrooms, and real swings with seats, not some old tire."

Nobody was impressed. *Leave it to Gina to get off on the wrong foot,* Izzy thought. Then it was Alex's turn. He stood up, faced the room and smiled at everyone. "I'm Alexander Gamboli, Alex for short. My sister and I live in the old Simpson house off the road behind the woods. It's kind of run-down, but we're fixing it up. I like it here in the country."

The little girls titter. The older girls smiled back. Alex made a big hit with everyone.

During the introductions, Izzy had time to put her supplies in her desk and look around. In the very front row was Janet in a new dress. Izzy didn't recognize her at first because the golden spiral curls no longer hung to her shoulders. Instead, her hair was pulled back in a gentle wave and flipped under at the neck in the new pageboy style. It still looked like gold in the sunlight.

Miss Webb called the first class: "Eighth grade arithmetic." Mike, Janet, and Izzy headed for the recitation bench. Alex looked confused. *He probably went to one of those big schools where every one in the room is in the same grade, and they don't go up front for their classes,* Izzy thought. When she passed his desk, she motioned for him to come on. "This is the way we do it here."

The bench was only big enough for three, so Alex volunteered to get one of the visitor chairs from the back of the room. Because Mike was the biggest of the four, he took the chair. Alex ended up between Janet and Izzy. Izzy felt uncomfortable but didn't know why.

At recess, Izzy could hardly wait to ask Janet about the hair. "I'm too old for those silly spiral curls. I want to look grown-up." Janet patted her new hairdo.

At noon, Izzy decided to stay in the building and eat her dinner at her desk while she worked on the morning's assignments. That way, she wouldn't have to take them home. Outside, she heard the rest of the kids having a great time. She wondered, *what is Gina doing, and is Alex flirting with Janet?*

At quarter to one, her lessons finished, she headed for the outhouse. Through the closed door, she heard voices. Inside, Janet and Irene were talking. Izzy knew that there were only two holes her size, so she waited.

"I don't think Izzy is interested in being president anymore," Janet said. "I tried to show her the swell constitution I wrote, and she was too busy showing Mr. Smart-Alex a broken down bicycle she was trying to fix. She's always bragging about how she wants to be an engineer. That's stupid. Girls can't be engineers."

Irene agreed. Izzy ducked behind the outhouse, so they wouldn't know she had heard them.

That afternoon, when Alex brought his mother to see Ma, he told Izzy that Janet was telling everyone on the playground that Izzy was against the swell constitution she had spent all summer writing and that Izzy shouldn't be president. Izzy laughed. "Why, that sneaky little so-and-so. I never said a word to put it down."

"Hey, I'm still an outsider here. I'm not getting mixed up in your politics."


Friday afternoon arrived. President Izzy took her seat at the teacher's desk with Secretary/Treasurer Janet beside her.

Tap, tap, tap.

Izzy rapped her knuckles on the desk and brought the meeting to order. After the minutes were read, she announced that nominations were open for president for the coming year.

"I nominate Isabelle Norton," Jack said. Someone seconded the nomination.

"Are there any other nominations?" Izzy asked.

"I nominate Janet Andrews," Irene said.

*I'm not surprised*, Izzy thought.

Someone seconded the nomination. Then the nominations were closed. Izzy put the vice president, Jim, in charge of the meeting, while she and Janet went outside. They stood on the step, but neither one said anything. It seemed forever before Horace popped his head out the door and told them to come back in.

"The vote was a tie. We voted three times." Jim told them. "Then, we voted to decide the elections by flipping a coin. Izzy is president now, so Janet, you call heads or tails while the coin is in the air."

Just as Jim tossed a penny, Izzy grabbed it and said, "No, let Janet have it. I really need to be free from the duty, to be able to spend more time with my mother." There was a polite applause. Izzy didn't know if it was for her or for Janet, but they shook hands, and she took her seat in the back.

Janet tapped lightly with her knuckles on the desk, and the meeting continued.

Izzy let her mind wander. She thought about Ma and the new baby. *I hope we're ready before it comes. We have only a few baby clothes, blankets, and diapers and a worn-out homemade cradle. Maybe I can borrow Janet's book to see what else we need.*

She heard them elect Jim vice president again and Irene, secretary/treasurer. Then Janet brought up the constitution. She read, and read, and read. Soon, the little kids became restless. Before long, some of the kids started arguing about different things. Izzy's mind was elsewhere.

Everyone in the room seemed to be talking at once. Janet called for order, but nobody paid any attention. She rapped her knuckles and raised her voice. Still, the hubbub continued.

Janet's face turned pink, then red. Finally, she stood up and shouted, "Shut up!"

She grabbed a bottle of ink and slammed it down on the desk to get attention.

There was total silence.

Ink and blood ran off the desk onto the floor.

# Chapter 41

When Izzy saw the blood, she rushed to the front and almost ran into Miss Webb. The teacher took the first-aid box from the bottom drawer and spoke to the classroom full of startled children.

"I'm disappointed in all of you. Please be quiet as you leave. We'll discuss this Monday morning." Her voice remained calm, but her hands shook as she wrapped Janet's injured hand.

Izzy wiped up the desk and the floor with wads of paper from the wastebasket. *It's a good thing all our papers were in her briefcase and not on the desk.* Then, she helped the teacher take Janet to her car.

On Monday morning, twenty subdued students sat up very straight, listening to Miss Webb. "I said we would discuss

Friday's behavior this morning. When everyone talks at the same time, they are not listening to others' ideas. When Janet tapped for order, she meant 'be quiet'. She's the president now, and she has the right to say who will talk during the meeting. If you have something that you think will be helpful, raise your hand. When she calls your name, you may talk."

Janet sat at her desk with a smug half-grin on her face. Her right hand had a bandage, and she held it on her shoulder, so that everyone in the room could see she had been hurt.

"I thought about it this weekend," the teacher continued. "We'll take a half-hour right now. The first grade will take a piece of paper and write from one to ten, ten times. The second grade will write from one to one hundred. Third and fourth grade will write this sentence a hundred times." She walked to the blackboard and wrote "I will only talk at meetings when called on by the president."

"Fifth through eighth will write a one-page essay on proper conduct at meetings."

Gina raised her hand. "I wasn't talking last Friday. Do I have to write that?"

"It's good that you weren't talking. You can write a page on making friends in a new community."

She turned her back to go to her desk and, almost as an afterthought, turned. "By the way, there will be no recesses today, to account for the time needed to do your extra assignment."

# Chapter 42

At the end of September, the weather turned cold, but no rain came. Pa built a fire in the heating stove and moved Ma's bed into the sitting room so she could keep warm.

One afternoon, Janet and her mother arrived at the Norton's house with a box wrapped in tissue paper and tied with a yellow ribbon.

When Mrs. Andrews handed it to Ma, Janet announced that, since they didn't know if it was going to be a boy or a girl, they chose yellow, which could be for either sex. Ma thanked them as she opened the box. There was a beautiful, hand-knit yellow sweater, two tiny booties, and a knit bonnet.

"I made the bonnet," Janet said. "Granny taught me how to knit this summer when she visited us. She made the booties and Mother did the sweater."

"That's very nice of you, they are lovely" Ma told her. "I know the baby won't care about the color as long as it is warm."

While Ma and Mrs. Andrews talked, Izzy and Janet sat on the couch.

"Izzy, I'm sorry I treated you so mean. I had no idea that your ma was having such a rough time of it." Izzy couldn't remember Janet ever saying she was sorry about anything.

"Oh, that's okay. I was sure shocked when she told me. I didn't want another brother or sister, but now that the time is getting closer, I can hardly wait. I have gotten pretty good at taking care of Ma, and the Gambolis have been so kind. They bring us something for supper almost every day."

"Are you sweet on Alex?" Janet asked.

"I don't think so, but he likes the same stuff I do, like engines and airplanes and stuff."

"Oh, Izzy, you're such a tomboy. Don't you ever think about pretty dresses and hairstyles?"

"Sometimes, but what good would it do? I'm not very good at that sort of stuff. By the way, I think you did a great job on the constitution. I don't blame you for thinking I didn't like it. I did, but had my mind on other things?"

"Thank you. I studied the Constitution all summer. I even read the Federalist Papers. I've decided I'm going to be a lawyer."

"Hey, that's great. You can help me get patents on my inventions if I ever get a chance to invent anything."

The girls laughed and hugged each other.

# Chapter 43

One day, when Izzy got home, a strange car stood in the driveway. Izzy heard Pa and a stranger in the kitchen talking quietly to each other. Not wanting to interrupt them, she waited on the porch. She put her ear close to the door and listened. She only made out a few words. The man wanted to give Pa some money to let his friends use the woods for hunting and to keep everyone else out. When she heard the chairs scrape on the kitchen floor, she made a lot of noise as though she had just come home.

"Isabelle, this is Sheriff Jones," Pa said, as he and the man came out the door.

A few evenings later, when she came into the kitchen to get Ma's supper tray, she heard Bud arguing with Pa.

"But why can't we hunt in our woods?" Bud's face was red, and he looked angry.

"Because—I said so." Whenever Pa said that, Izzy and Bud knew it was the end of the conversation.

By early October, light frost decorated the dead weeds and grass around the farm yard. "Pa, I don't think those rich guys you're letting hunt in our wood are hunters. I never hear any shots fired." Bud grumped around the house and made Izzy uneasy.

# Chapter 44

"I've been having pains in the back every hour or so all day," Ma told Izzy when she came in one day after school. "Your pa says they're probably just false labor pains. But Pa's never had a baby, and I have, so I know what labor pains feel like." Ma rolled on her side and asked Izzy to rub her back for two or three minutes.

After supper, the family sat around the gasoline lamp in the sitting room, reading, while Ma tossed and turned in the bed. At last Pa threw his paper down and paced around the room, picking up little items and putting them down.

Finally he said, "Sheriff Jones came here this afternoon. Tonight is the night. They expect the Gamboli truck back from Canada full of booze. It has been gone for three days. The sheriff's men have been watching that place for the last few weeks. He thinks the runner will be coming to pick up their loads tonight."

"You mean that nice Mrs. Gamboli is involved in something like that? I don't believe it." Ma shook her head from side to side and frowned.

"I didn't want to believe it either. I guess I was selfish, hoping it wasn't so because I liked all that good food. But I knew we couldn't cut it off, or they would think something was going on."

"You all need to know the plan," Pa told them. "We are to lock and guard the doors. The sheriff thinks they might try to hole up here and use us as hostages. He says to put out the bright light and pull the shades. The sheriff wants Bud and me upstairs with our guns. They expect them to come over the hill and through our pasture to get away.

The Feds will have their men on top of our windmill and on the roofs of the barn, the shed, and the granary. We are not to open the doors and only shoot at their feet if they try to get in the house." He lit the kerosene lamp and turned off the bright gasoline lamp. Bud and Izzy pulled all the shades.


Ma let out a little scream. "Oh! Oh! Oh! That one was real."

About twenty minutes later, Ma screamed again, louder. "Norman, this is no false pain. I'm in labor."

"You can't be. The baby isn't due until next month."

"Well, I'm in labor, call Doctor Hull."

"Let's wait until the pains are a little closer. I don't think the doctor wants to sit around here and get caught in a gunfight."

Ma let out a longer, louder scream. Bud jumped up. "I'll get the 22 and guard the front door." He disappeared.

"Oh, all right, I'll call him. Then I'll get the shotgun and go upstairs and watch the kitchen door. Izzy, stay with your ma," Pa barked.

Twenty minutes later, Ma quit screaming and started grunting.

Just as Ma relaxed and quit grunting, the phone rang. Izzy let go of Ma's hand and dashed to the kitchen to answer it.

"Hello, is that you, Izzy? This is Dr. Hull. I'm at Mr. Turner's place. I can't get to your house because the sheriff has the road blocked. Where's your pa?"

"He's upstairs with the shotgun guarding the back door. The sheriff told him they'll raid the Gamboli place tonight and not to let anyone come in the door until he comes back and says it's okay."

"Are you alone with your ma?"

"I was 'till you called."

"Go back to her, and don't leave her for anything. You're a big girl so listen carefully. How often are her pains coming?"

"About every five minutes."

"Okay. When she has a pain, tell her to try not to bear down and to pant like a dog instead. Watch between her legs, and if you see the top of the baby's head coming out, don't try to hold it back. Just take a clean towel and hold the bottom of the head. Let it ease out slowly. Have you got that?"

"I think so. I'm scared."

"Well, just take a deep breath, and do what you have to. Now, when the head is out, the baby will start to turn. Gently, very gently, push down on the top of the head with the other hand underneath it. When the top shoulder comes out, gently lift up, and the other shoulder will come out. Let the rest of the baby flop into your hand. She's not due yet, so it should come out without any problems. Now, the most important part, take the baby by both ankles. It will be a little slippery. Be sure to get a good grip, and hold it up with the head down and gently rub its back from the hips to the head. That will force a lot of liquid out of its mouth. If the baby starts to breathe, that's good. If it doesn't, give it a little slap on its bottom."

"Yes, Doctor, I'll try. I'm so scared."

"It's all right to be scared, but just do as I've told you." He sounded kind but very firm.

"As soon as the baby is breathing and gets red, wrap it up in the towel and put it on your ma's tummy with the head down and turned to the side. I'll be there just as soon as they let me. I'll take care of everything else. You'll do fine. Now get back to your ma."

Just as she got back to the sitting room, Ma started grunting again. Izzy told her not to push but pant like a dog. After two or three more contractions, as Izzy watched, she saw a patch of hair about the size of a small potato.

"Oh, Ma, its coming! Pant, pant, don't bear down!"

Twice more, Ma grunted and then panted. And each time, the patch of hair got bigger.

"Oh! Oh! Here it comes!" Ma called.

Izzy held the towel below the head just as it popped out. All she could see was the top of the head and a large patch of dark hair. *What did he say to do now?*

Her hands shook. Without any help from Izzy, the tiny head turned to the left, and she saw the baby's face. *Now I remember: let it turn, and gently push down on the top of the head.*

"Oh! Oh! The shoulder is out!"

She lifted the head up and, sure enough, the other shoulder and the rest of the baby just fell into her hands. She grasped its tiny feet at the ankles with her left hand and almost dropped it because it was so slippery and had white gunk all over it. When she held it up with its head hanging down, Ma rose up on her elbows, as Izzy stroked the tiny back.

In the dim light, Izzy thought it looked a little blue and gave it a whack on its bottom. She whacked it a little harder than she thought she should but heard a soft cry.

# Chapter 45

Just as the baby started crying, they heard a loud crash out back and chickens squawking. It sounded like a truck coming right through the hen house. Izzy quickly wrapped up the baby and plopped it on Ma's belly with its head lower than its shoulders. Then she fell on Ma and hugged her.

Izzy held one hand on the baby's back and felt the little heart beating away and the tiny chest expanding and contracting. Ma's hand lay below hers, over the butt and legs.

Shots rang out from the back of the house.

Mother and daughter held tight to each other and the baby. It may have been five minutes or an hour. They were too frightened to know. Then they heard a man shouting at the kitchen door. "It's good hunting tonight, Norton. Let me in." *That must be the sheriff using their code sentence.* Pa and Bud came lumbering down the stairs. Bud dashed into the kitchen to light a lamp and unlock the door. Pa rushed into the sitting room, followed by Dr. Hull.

Pa took the towel off the baby and lifted it up just a little. "Nellie, it's a girl, and she's alive and breathing!"

He quickly covered her back up and gave Ma a long kiss. Izzy realized that this was a special moment for them and headed for the kitchen. The doctor followed her.

"Is the baby okay?" Izzy looked at the kind face of the doctor. "She's so tiny."

"She's probably only eight months, but she looks good. You did a great job Isabelle. We need to keep her nice and warm."

"They always say to boil water when a baby comes, so I boiled two kettles full. They're on the back of the stove and are probably cold now, though," she told him.

"That's great, Izzy. It should be just about the right temperature. I can use it to wash my hands and clean up the baby and your ma."

When Izzy and the doctor came into the kitchen, it was full of men, all talking at once. Bud poked up the fire in the stove. Izzy washed her hands and made a fresh pot of coffee.

"We got a bunch of them," someone said. Everyone was shouting and happy.

"Yeah, I saw cars burning all over the area," said another.

When she looked out the open door, the first thing she saw was the Gamboli truck blazing away. She saw two men carrying a box, heading for the open door. Then she saw a bright red glow behind the woods in the direction of the Gamboli's house.

"Alex! What happened to Alex?"

"Who's Alex?" asked Sheriff Jones.

"He's Izzy's boyfriend," Bud told them. "He's old man Gamboli's son."

"I think one car got away. Maybe he was driving. There were three people in the front of that coupe that sped west through that bare field, out of range and over the hill," the sheriff said.

"Hey, Dave," a man shouted. "How come you didn't shoot the black coupe?"

"There were two kids and an old woman in that car. They may be gangsters, but no one is going to say that 'Dead-Eye Dave' has to shoot old women and kids to put notches on his rifle."

"That would be his mother and his sister." Izzy wanted to hug the burly lawman. *I hope they move to a nice big city with an airport. Alex can learn to fly and Gina can be happy. I'll tell Ma that their mother is okay too.*

Just then, they heard a series of muffled explosions as the truck fire reached the whiskey and caused the bottles to blow up.

"We salvaged one case of high-grade Canadian Whiskey for evidence before we put a bullet in the truck tank," said a man, taking a bottle from the box. "This one is for the guy that owns the barn."

"We had a perfect shot when that big, old truck came right though one of those buildings out there," said the second man.

"Great," shouted Bud, reaching for the bottle.

"Not so fast, young man; Do you own this place?" one man asked.

Izzy grabbed the bottle. "I'll take it to Pa. He's in the sitting room with our ma. She just had a baby."

"A man out there said this is for you, Pa."

In the dim light, Ma saw the label. "Oh! No! We can't accept it. It's illegal."

Pa took the bottle. "Of course not, we'll give it to Dr. Hull—for medicinal use of course."

The doctor laughed and accepted the bottle, as he made room for it in the bottom of his black bag.

The baby, wrapped in a blanket, nestled in Ma's arm. Pa looked all proud and happy. On the floor, Izzy saw a basin full of something that looked like a fresh liver, right after butchering. "What is that?" she asked.

"That's the afterbirth," the doctor told her. "The baby gets its nourishment through the cord attached to its belly button. It's called the placenta, and it grew on the wall of your mother's womb until after the baby was born. Then it came out. In the morning, your pa can bury it under a rosebush in the yard."

"That's it, Norman," Ma shouted. "We'll name her Rose."

"The human body is the most wonderful machine the good Lord ever designed," the doctor said. "It's a great privilege to be allowed to help keep it in tip-top shape and to help new babies into the world."

"You should think about being a nurse, Isabelle, or maybe, later, even a doctor. Some women are becoming doctors now, you know. You did a great job here tonight. Now, I think I should go see if any of those lawmen or the men in the truck needs my help."

# Chapter 46

Everything finally became quiet. *It must be almost morning,* Izzy thought, as she crawled into bed, still wearing her overalls. What the doctor had said burned in her brain.

*Nurse—Doctor—Engineer—which will it be? It costs so much money to be an engineer. Money we won't have when I get out of high school. I'll bet it costs a lot to be a doctor too. But they say nurses' training is really cheap, because the students learn while taking care of patients in the hospital. I've heard that registered nurses make good money. If I could get to be a registered nurse, I could work and earn a lot of money.*

*I liked taking care of Ma and got a real thrill helping baby Rose get born. Maybe later, I could go to the university to be a doctor—or an engineer, and I could invent stuff for doctors.*

Henry's crow woke her up. Still groggy from the long, exciting night, she thought it sounded a little funny. She finally roused herself and looked out the window.

The whole flock of chickens were staggering and falling down around the burned out truck where all those bottles of whiskey had blown up.